A
Deeper Darkness

Alby Stone

Copyright © 2019 Alby Stone

All rights reserved.

ISBN: 9781793384393

The winds were wither'd in the stagnant air,
And the clouds perish'd; Darkness had no need
Of aid from them – She was the Universe.

– Lord Byron, *Darkness*, 1816.

1

Trees in every direction, nothing but trees. Birch, alder, rowan, aspen. A sprinkling of larch and pine on higher ground. Others he couldn't name and didn't care to know. He was heartily sick of trees. And so damned weary. Tired to the bone and fed up to the back teeth with what had once been a simple but important pleasure. Like thousands of other young Germans he had spent his summers in woodland camps, overjoyed to be away from the city and surrounded by nature. Long hikes across pasture and through forest, swimming naked in rivers and tarns, dutifully singing songs he didn't really understand as he marched with his fellows through the Fatherland's leafy natural treasures. Sunny days in the drab plumage of a Wandervogel, a more innocent uniform than the one he later came to wear. Then those two precious summers with his best friend, rambling and cycling in France, Belgium, Denmark, the Netherlands and England, working on farms to pay for food, shelter in inclement weather, and whatever transport their feet or bicycles couldn't handle.

But he'd been a child then, in all but years. War had changed him, shown him truths that sent the inner boy screaming for his lost mother, leaving only the hollowed, disillusioned man. And this wilderness of unruly brown and green was simply depressing. Now the only trees he wanted to see were those that had been tamed into tables and chairs, doors and walls. All he wanted was to be surrounded by buildings, with cobblestones underfoot and beer in his hand. Motor cars, gramophone records and laughter; books, newspapers and cinemas; a soft, clean bed and the touch of a woman's hand. Something honest and true from before all this.

Jochen stopped walking and held up a hand, surveyed the vaguely triangular glade then turned to face the men trailing behind him. 'Right, that's enough for today. We'll make camp here. I know it's early but we've come a long way and I think we all need a damned good rest. You know what to do.' He sat on a mossy rock, removed his boots and lit an Eckstein. Smoking was frowned upon in the Reich, but what the hell. If an occasional cigar was good enough for Reichsmarschall Hermann Göring, a cigarette was good enough for Hauptsturmführer Jochen Dietrich.

A man sat heavily beside him, shaking his head when Jochen offered him a smoke. 'No thanks. I can barely breathe as it is. The tents can wait five fucking minutes. I'm sodding well exhausted and I need to get the weight off my poor sore feet for a bit. They feel like two lumps of Milbenkäse, and I swear the fucking mites are still nibbling at them. And these bastard trousers chafe like hell. No wonder the Ivans are such miserable sods. My balls will be worn down to the size of peas by the time we've finished doing whatever the fuck we're here to do.'

It wasn't the subtlest of hints, and it was by no means the first. Jochen grinned at his old friend. 'I honestly don't know, Rudi. Hrubesch and Berger will tell us when get nearer, and I have no idea when that will be. I have my orders, they have theirs.'

'From Himmler in person, so rumour has it.'

'The rumour is true, according to Hrubesch. Not that he told me anything more than roughly where we were being sent. I have no idea what the mission is actually about. As I said, I'll be told what we're supposed to achieve when we get to wherever the hell we're going.'

'Why are those two Ahnenerbe freaks so important? Why tell them but not you?'

'If that's what Berger and Hrubesch really are. And please don't bother asking them. They'd probably reveal that they're really generals and order me to shoot you.'

Rudi laughed sourly. 'If it puts an end to this bloody chafing, I'm all for it. But could they really order you to do that? I thought you were in charge of this mission.'

'Security, transport and supplies,' Jochen sighed. 'I'm basically chief bodyguard to those freaks, and the rest of you are my hopefully obedient henchmen. Once we get there, wherever *there* is, they'll be running the show.'

Rudi nodded. 'Assuming there is a show at all. I'd bet a year's shitty pay that this turns out to be another of Heinrich fucking Himmler's crazy pipe dreams. They say he's sent teams out to look for the Holy Grail, the Spear of Destiny, Aaron's Rod, the Urim and Thummim, and the Ark of the Covenant. For a man who hates Jews so much he seems a bit overly obsessed with Hebrew stuff, if you ask me. Maybe he should be wearing a yellow star.'

'Careful what you say, my friend. And who you say it to.'

'Don't worry, Jochen. I know who to trust. And that's none of those blokes over yonder. They're all fanatics. Sell you down the fucking river without a second thought if they believed it served the Reich. And I'm pretty sure that arsehole Karnstein is a plant. SD, I reckon.'

'Sicherheitsdienst?' Jochen was sceptical. 'Spying on an SS operation? You really think so?'

'They spy on everyone, you know that. I wouldn't be surprised if they watch Adolf when he takes a dump, just to make sure his arse isn't treacherously passing secrets to the British.'

'Keep your voice down.'

'They're too far away to hear,' said Rudi airily, helping himself to an Eckstein from Jochen's pack. 'Christ, I wish we were back in Rangoon. That was lovely. Good weather, passable beer and decent grub. I hate this poxy place. It reminds me of the Ukraine. And that is one place I'm never going to visit again. We were fucking lucky there, even with everything that happened.' He nodded toward the camp now being assembled. 'If those bastards knew what we did…'

'Well, they won't hear it from me. Christ, Rudi – how did we get into this mess?'

'Survival, mate. Anyway, it was your bright idea. That sudden conversion from idealistic commie to heel-clicking Nazi when you saw which way the wind was blowing. And I was stupid enough to go along with it.'

'As I recall, it was your idea. Besides, things were different then. Neither of us thought all that sabre-rattling would actually lead to war, and certainly not a war like this. Anyway, we didn't have the money to get out of Germany and make a fresh start in another country, and if we had we'd have been interned as enemy aliens. We'd both be dead or rotting in a prison by now if we hadn't switched sides.'

'True,' said Rudi. 'But quite honestly, these sodding strides are chafing so much I'm not sure death wouldn't have been a better option. Though I'll keep an open mind about the prison trousers. Look, there's no point at all in worrying about the rights and wrongs of what we did getting on for ten years ago. We both thought the situation in Germany would calm down once the thugs had got the resentment out of their system and the economy improved. We thought all that Lebensraum stuff was political hot air, the usual empty tub-thumping. I for one didn't dream mad Adolf would want to take over Austria and the Sudetenland, let alone Poland. And yes, my idea of joining the SS was a mistake. Shit, I thought we'd just be the Führer's bodyguard, not expanded into a parallel army and ordered to do unspeakable things. Who the fuck could have predicted how crazy it would get? But I guess we're living proof of Moltke's maxim that no plan survives first contact with the enemy's main strength, which in this case just happened to be blaming everyone but ourselves for our self-inflicted damage, offering Jew-free jam today, and making Germany great again. Our precarious position also amply demonstrates the limits of our own morality, Jochen. Kierkegaard and Schopenhauer were right about Kant's so-called categorical imperative. Humanity may be bound by the moral law it imposes upon itself, but laws are both subject to change and usually for the benefit of the people who have the power to make those changes. Like our own plan, Kant's imperative is subject to Moltke's maxim. It doesn't survive first contact with ego, self-interest, delusion and hubris. Basically, the forces of light are only effective until someone flips the switch. But enough of that. If we happen to bump into the Red Army out here, we can both stop worrying about our little ethical dilemma.'

That was typical Rudi. He was as foul-mouthed as a drunken fishwife and liked to affect coarseness, but occasionally his erudition showed through the mask. Jochen sighed again. 'Come on, we'd better lend a hand with the camp. Look at the mess Hrubesch and Berger are making. Those idiots look as if they've never pitched a tent in their lives. Every night I have to show them how to do it, and they never learn.'

'That's because they're human, Jochen. And that explains precisely why we are here and now, somewhere in the middle of bloody Siberia with a global war raging and another bloodthirsty madman in charge of our once-lovely country. Humans never fucking learn.' Rudi stood and gazed around him. 'Fucking Siberia,' he grumbled. 'This is no place for a good German boy.'

'You're not a good boy and we've been in worse. Anyway, there are noble precedents for Germans wandering around out here. In the 1700s the naturalist Peter Simon Pallas spent six years exploring the area between the Urals and Lake Baikal.'

Rudi spat out one of the ubiquitous Siberian midges.

'Little bastards. Yes, I know a bit about Pallas. Found a big meteorite with a new mineral and named it after himself. Discovered a cat that nobody had ever seen except the people who live here and knew all about it. Didn't name it after them, I notice. But he wasn't sent on a fool's errand by that arsehole Himmler, was he?'

'We don't know it's a fool's errand,' Jochen pointed out.

Rudi laughed. 'If Himmler sent us, then that's exactly what it is.'

'Less of that talk, Obersturmführer Brandt. You'll get us transferred to the Eastern Front.'

'Been there, done that, didn't like it. But at least we'd be a bit closer to home,' said Rudi gloomily. 'Where are we now, do you reckon?'

'About three hundred and fifty kilometres north of Krasnoyarsk, according to Berger. The middle of nowhere's middle of nowhere. Other than that, I haven't a clue. Berger is mapping as we go, with Karnstein's help, but frankly I wouldn't put too much faith in their or anyone else's cartography in this wilderness. It's all trees and ferns and rocks as far as the eye can see, no unique salient features whatsoever. Hrubesch says we'll probably need to turn northeast in another day or two, maybe three.'

'Hrubesch.' Rudi grimaced. 'I cannot believe we're relying on his method to navigate this shit-hole. Dead-reckoning, a compass or a sextant, following the sun and stars, fine. But holding a lump of rock on a chain over a blank piece of paper? You must be fucking joking.'

'It's meteoric iron, apparently, from a site in Greenland. Hrubesch says he can attune his mind to the target and channel the signal through the chain and into the stone, which then shows which direction we ought to take.'

'Bollocks,' Rudi jeered. 'Fucking mumbo-jumbo. Do you believe that?'

'I've seen Charlie Chaplin's long-lost twin brother become Führer and pick a fight with the rest of the world,' said Jochen. 'I can now believe almost anything at all except that this is going to end well.'

Rudi nodded glumly. 'No arguing with that, mate. You know, I thought last year was bad but this is turning out to be a *really* shit year.'

Jochen Dietrich and Rudolf Brandt were both twenty-nine years of age, with Jochen the elder by a couple of days short of two months. They'd lived two streets apart in Leipzig, attended the same schools, played for the same junior football team. They were practically brothers and in fact were often taken as siblings, even though they didn't look much alike. Rudi was a few centimetres taller, fine-featured and handsome, with the SS-approved blond hair and blue eyes. Jochen was presentable but plain, with acceptable green eyes and a reddish tint to his sandy locks. He was quiet, reserved and thoughtful where Rudi was outgoing, noisy and an incorrigible gossip. Yet their closeness made them seem more alike than they were, and Jochen's careful consideration neatly complemented Rudi's impetuosity. Where one went, the other usually followed. Rudi had dutifully accompanied Jochen when his social ideals and Wandervogel spirit led him to the fringes of the local Communist Party – ironically but luckily, they'd been too poor to pay the subscription so never formally joined – and in 1936 Jochen had gone along with Rudi's eminently sensible notion that it would be safer within the Nazi Party than outside it. Then the war began, and they'd somehow followed each other into the Schutzstaffel, where they fought together and rose a little way through the ranks as senior officers were promoted or died. But fighting seemed increasingly less of a patriotic duty and more of a senseless slaughter. Then came the Ukrainian horror that had somehow elevated them to their present positions.

Jochen didn't like to think about that. When he did, he consoled himself with the knowledge that they had committed one atrocity to prevent a greater evil. He remembered Rudi's pale but sweaty face, the astonished expressions of their victims as they fell, the tears and pleas for a mercy Jochen was unable to give. Rudi's words of hate and contempt when he put a bullet into the head of the brutal man whose rank Jochen now held: *I didn't join up to shoot unarmed women and children, you fucking piece of shit.*

He stared into the campfire, ignoring the low murmur of the Ahnenerbe eggheads, the louder banter of the other men, Rudi among them. When this war was over, how would he be called to account? As a traitor or a war criminal? He supposed it would depend on which side was victorious and how thorough their investigations were, how conscientious. In the confusion of war, many things were missed or overlooked, even by the Third Reich's irresistible bureaucracy and obsessive cataloguing. But in the aftermath blame and retribution would hold sway. Would it be the ever-suspicious Nazis, with their meticulous, forensic attention to detail and a veritable army of spies, informers and inquisitors? The British or Americans, who might give him a fair if stern hearing before consigning him to the gallows? Or the Soviets, who would surely shoot him on sight? Whoever won, scapegoats would be sought, found and punished. There would be mistakes and the niceties of justice would not be a priority. There would be a reckoning, a visceral need for blame and vengeance. Retribution would be exacted and seen to be done. Show trials and mass executions. An eye for an eye and a tooth for a tooth would be the very least of it.

Jochen was not optimistic. But at that moment he had to focus on getting this job done and staying alive long enough to get back to Germany. There was no point facing the music until the orchestra had finished tuning up.

2

The next evening, Hrubesch took Jochen aside and told him it was time to change direction. 'Tomorrow morning we turn northeast. My pendulum indicates we are approaching the target.'

Privately, Jochen didn't believe the pendulum could do anything but turn in little circles at the behest of Hrubesch's wishful thinking. Its workings had never been explained. 'I don't suppose your magic stone told how much further we have to walk? My feet are killing me.'

Hrubesch shrugged. 'It shouldn't be far. Perhaps another three days. But we are close. The pendulum is reacting strongly.'

'Good,' said Jochen, feigning cheerfulness. 'And did it also tell you how and where we're going to find food? Our field rations are low. The mission plan depended on supplementing them with game but there's none to be had. I estimate we have another week until we're eating our boots. Or the mules. Or each other.'

Hrubesch ignored Jochen's sarcasm. 'We shall do no such thing. If necessary, we can hunt.'

'Weren't you listening? There's nothing here to hunt. The forest should be teeming with wildlife but I haven't seen so much as a mouse in the last few days. Just these bloody midges.'

'I suspect that, too is another sign that we are near.'

'Near to what? When are you going to tell me what we are doing in this Godforsaken wilderness?'

'The pendulum will tell me when the time is right. Until then, carry out your orders. Maintain the security of this mission.'

A sudden thought struck Jochen. 'You and Berger aren't Ahnenerbe, are you? Well, obviously you are – you wouldn't have much pull with the Waffen-SS otherwise. But you're something else as well. The Ahnenerbe may do a lot of research into weird stuff, but I've never actually met one who uses magic.'

'The pendulum is not magic,' said Hrubesch loftily. 'It operates on purely scientific principles. Radiaesthesia, a true Germanic science, which recognises that a man's will is as much a physical force as gravity and can be attuned to resonate with another person or object. I meditate upon the target and adjust the length of the chain until the bob resonates with both target and its direction. A simple process, but one which requires a superior will. That is how a man with a forked hazel twig may find water, and why the Führer can do the things he has done, bending the German people to his will, and so revealing to them their destiny. And that is what is so often mistaken for magic by weak and ignorant minds – the power of the superior man's will.'

Oh, wonderful. Another bloody madman. And this one doubles as an arrogant, pompous idiot. 'If you say so,' said Jochen tiredly. Hrubesch had not replied to his question about the Ahnenerbe, but that could wait. 'I'm just a humble soldier. What the hell do I know?'

Jochen returned to the camp and began methodically disassembling and cleaning his Luger and MP 40 submachine gun, and the battered Great War vintage Lee-Enfield rifle he could carry openly. When he'd put the firearms back together, reloaded them and stowed the MP 40 alongside the other items in his kitbag – my German bag, he thought wryly – he tucked the pistol into the back of the coarse working trousers he wore and went in search of Rudi.

His friend was playing cards with the flint-eyed Karnstein and two younger Sturmmänner whose names Jochen could not bring to mind. The pile of cigarettes nearest Rudi told Jochen his friend was enjoying a good run of luck.

'What are you playing?'

'Skat,' said Rudi without looking up. 'And I'm doing rather well.'

Karnstein glared up at his Hauptsturmführer. 'It's these damned cards,' he complained. 'I'm from Cologne. We have clubs, diamonds and spades, proper suits, not this yokel shit. I mean, acorns and leaves? Bells? By the time I've worked out what I've got, that jammy bastard's already beaten me.'

'That jammy bastard is your Obersturmführer, Sturmmann Karnstein. Show some respect.'

'He's got my smokes and now you want me to give

him my respect too? Fuck that.'

Jochen squatted on his haunches. 'Listen to me, Karnstein. We are behind enemy lines and it is imperative that we are not identified. That is why we are not maintaining the full discipline that would otherwise be expected of a Schutzstaffel unit. Heel-clicking and straight-arm salutes would give us away as surely as a swastika armband. Our orders are to *appear* to be itinerant Soviet workers. That does not mean that you are free to go around bad-mouthing your superiors. Is that clear? Now apologise to the Obersturmführer, or when we get back home you'll find yourself on a charge.'

For a moment Jochen though Karnstein was going to challenge him. He carefully snaked his right hand to the small of his back and gripped the Luger tightly, readying himself to pull it out of his waistband and pull the trigger. He wasn't too bothered about shooting someone like Karnstein. It wouldn't be the first time. At least this one would be justifiable by SS standards.

Karnstein grinned, though the murderous glint didn't leave his eyes. 'Yes, sir. Of course. I wouldn't want to jeopardise the mission in any way. Obersturmführer Brandt, I apologise.'

'Accepted,' said Rudi, his smile marginally less sincere than Karnstein's apology.

'Good,' said Jochen. 'Right, that's enough Skat for tonight. And Obersturmführer, give those cigarettes back to whichever of these fools lost them. Get some sleep, all of you. We have another bloody long day tomorrow.'

It had been a long journey even before they had to start

walking. Two weeks at a secret camp in the Black Forest, learning how to look and behave like Soviet fur trappers, hunters and foragers; being taught a smattering of Russian and the rudiments of the Cyrillic alphabet; poring over mostly empty maps of Siberia. Their teachers were Ahnenerbe men, ethnologists and others who'd carried out fieldwork in the region before the Great War. Apparently, there were people living in the Siberian taiga who even after nearly thirty years of Marxist-Leninist progress were virtually unknown to the Soviet authorities: obscure tribes of nomadic reindeer-herders, isolated and secretive religious communities, outlaws and bandits, and misanthropic men who lived by trapping beaver, sable and wolf for their pelts. Berger and Hrubesch had been selected not only for their expertise in certain fields of which Jochen had not been apprised, but also for their supposed fluency in the Russian language.

After that, they were driven in a Wehrmacht truck to Kiel and loaded onto a U-boat. Weeks of cramped discomfort and tortuous evasion of Allied attention later, they arrived in Rangoon, where they enjoyed a blissful week of sunshine and fresh air. The Japanese – it came as no great surprise that Hrubesch also spoke their tongue – flew them in a Mitsubishi Ki-57 transport aircraft to a makeshift airfield in Manchuria, where they slipped across the border into the Soviet Union and travelled west on horseback to Krasnoyarsk, their equipment carried by half a dozen mules. The horses had been set free near an abandoned village to the north of Krasnoyarsk. Now all they had were the mules, with their mysterious burdens, and their feet.

The men – Jochen and Rudi aside – had been selected

on the basis of party loyalty and military prowess, naturally, but also physical strength and fitness, a record of resourcefulness under fire, and familiarity with horses. Only Jochen and Rudi had never ridden a horse before, so they'd been forced through a crash course in equestrianism. Jochen wasn't entirely sure why he'd been chosen to lead the soldiers and allowed to pick Rudi as his second-in-command. It may have been because of what had happened in the Ukraine. The yarn they'd spun to cover their arses had taken on a life of its own and resulted in each of the pair being awarded the Iron Cross, not to mention promotions and a brief spell as role models for aspiring psychopaths, name-checked by Joseph Goebbels and Himmler, lauded as paragons of Aryan manhood. They'd even been filmed by Leni Riefenstahl, though as far as Jochen knew none of the footage had yet found a way into one of her insufferable propaganda features. For that he was thankful.

He was rather less appreciative of the cyanide tablets wrapped in oilskin that nestled in his trouser pocket. They all had them, with orders to swallow one or two if it looked like they would be apprehended by the Soviets. Jochen was in two minds about that. Although horrified by the prospect of suicide, no matter how noble the cause – or how worthless – he knew the Soviets did not treat their prisoners well. And out here, in civilian dress, they would be considered spies. That meant a quick and relatively clean bullet in the head was out of the question. They would be interrogated, and from what Jochen had heard Soviet torturers were both brutal and ingenious. Even the Gestapo respected the NKVD questioning techniques, so Jochen had heard – though that had come from Rudi after a few beers, so he wouldn't necessarily take it as gospel.

Speaking of the devil, Rudi moved up alongside him. He seemed troubled. 'Have you seen anything?' he asked.

'Seen what?' Jochen replied.

'Not sure. I keep thinking I see something moving from the corner of my eye, but when I turn to look, it's gone. Saw it half a dozen times in the past couple of hours. Thought I was imagining things. Let's face it, this forest could drive anyone crazy. Then, when I went back to check on the men at the rear, I heard Bauer and Mann talking about it. Sounded like the same thing.'

Jochen could tell his friend was genuinely worried because he'd stopped swearing. 'What did it look like?'

'Just a quick flash of something white, maybe a pale grey. Like it comes out of the shadows and back again, so fast it's gone in a blink. Totally silent. Really put the wind up me. Hey, perhaps it's a bear.'

'This isn't the Arctic Circle. The bears here are black and brown, not grey or white. Could be wolves, I suppose. Though Christ knows what they live on in this Godforsaken wasteland.'

Rudi forced a grin. 'Let's hope it isn't Germans.'

'In that case they'd have all starved to death centuries ago. No, it isn't wolves, Rudi. There's nothing for them to eat here. There should be deer, boar, hares, all sorts of herbivores. That's why the taiga supports large predators like tigers, bears, wolves and lynx. We haven't seen any prey animals for days, not even birds. Nothing bigger than those damned midges.'

Rudi laughed heartily. 'Well, those little fuckers are

certainly getting plenty to eat. Obersturmführer Rudolf Brandt, mostly. Though to be fair, I'm getting my share of them. Whenever I inhale I must swallow a dozen or so of the buggers. My lungs must be fucking black with them. Still, enough go down the right pipe. They must be a little bit nutritious, surely.'

Jochen clapped him on the back. 'That's the spirit. You can do the same if a bear or a tiger crosses our path. Just open up and breathe it in.'

Rudi snapped off an ironically limp straight-arm salute. 'As you command, my beloved Hauptsturmführer. But don't worry. I'll save you the arse.'

That night, Karnstein reported that two of the men were unwell. When Jochen asked who they were, Karnstein told him the sick men were Sturmmänner Bauer and Mann. Jochen frowned. 'Weren't they the men taking up the rear today?'

'That's right, Hauptsturmführer.' Karnstein even managed to make his rank sound vaguely like an insult. 'They kept on about seeing things in the trees, something white. Must have been the start of whatever they've gone down with.'

They saw what Rudi thought he saw. I'll have to keep an eye on him. 'What are the symptoms?'

'Well, they've both been puking their guts up, can't keep anything down. Bauer's worse than Mann, though – he's got a pretty bad dose of the shits. He's in and out of those trees like a fiddler's elbow.'

'What else? High temperature? Sweating? Shivering?'

'That's what I expected, Hauptsturmführer. But when

Schaeffer took a look at them he said their temperatures were normal. No fever at all. Just really bad guts.'

'Perhaps they ate tainted meat. Those tins we're lugging around are vile at the best of times – frankly, I couldn't tell you what animal it came from or if it was off or not. And that Erbswurst is enough to liquidise anybody's bowels. Does anyone else feel unwell?'

Karnstein shook his head. 'Everyone else seems fine. Could it be the water?'

'Not likely, Karnstein. We've all been using water from the same streams and pools, and it's all been strained and boiled to kill germs before we use it for cooking and to fill our flasks. If it was some sort of chemical contamination, then we'd all be ill by now. I guess it could just be down to plain exhaustion. We've all walked a very long way carrying far too much, most of which is utterly useless as far as I can see.'

'I'm sure Reichsführer Himmler had his reasons.'

Jochen sighed. 'Yes, I expect he had.' *And none of them good or sane.*

When Karnstein had left, Jochen saw to his firearms as usual then, on impulse, turned out his bags. One bulky knapsack, now only partly filled with boxes of biscuit, tins of meat and Erbswurst, his last bottle of concentrated lemon juice, a tin of ersatz coffee, six cartons of Eckstein cigarettes. A fork and spoon, an enamel mug and billycan. Basic toiletries, a muslin bag for straining water. There had been much more when they started out, and it had been ridiculously heavy. It was no wonder his back ached all the time. But it hadn't been depleted much until they'd run out of deer to shoot. Low on food and, most worryingly, low on cigarettes. The return journey, if they made it that far, would not be joyous.

Then the canvas bag that looped over his shoulder. In that were ammunition for the Lee-Enfield, a hunting knife, a notebook and three pencils, a spare shirt, fake identity papers, and a wholly useless map of Siberia comprising mainly blank spaces.

The third and largest bag was the one that vexed him most sorely. It contained his MP 40, two extra magazines and ammunition for that, a box of rounds for the Luger, his real identity papers, and a sealed package containing what he'd been told was a full Hauptsturmführer's dress uniform, complete with jackboots, peaked cap, ceremonial dagger and his Iron Cross. And his very own special burden, a Nazi flag folded around a collapsible staff. All but the weapons utterly useless, as he reminded himself several times a day. At least he didn't have to cart a steel helmet around like the lower ranks.

A dress uniform? A swastika flag? They were liabilities, dead weight. His tent was more of the same – as senior officer he had it to himself but it only meant more weight to lug around. Rudi felt the same about his. The others had to share, which meant they could share the load. But it was expected. He had to keep himself separate from the lower ranks. Himmler's words haunted him with every twinge of protest from his lower back: *You may relax discipline to avoid suspicion but rank and purpose must be maintained at all times. When required you must present yourselves as exemplary soldiers and representatives of the Reich, ambassadors of the German people, the Aryan race.* At least they'd been on paper and not delivered in person. A small mercy.

Himmler. About as useful as the dress uniforms, the surplus tent. A man who believed in fantasies, fake science and melodramatic gestures, who thought nothing of sending eighteen supposedly invaluable SS men to baby-sit two ageing scientists on a protracted mission through enemy territory and into the middle of nowhere without telling them why they were going. Really, it was a miracle that they'd made it this far without even exchanging gunfire with the Soviets, let alone without losing anyone. No close contact with Soviet forces in all this time, only sporadic troop movements seen from afar near the border with Japanese-occupied Manchuria, a few distant trucks and horse-drawn wagons on dirt roads linking one remote settlement to the next. Nothing to the south of Irkutsk or as they skirted Krasnoyarsk. Jochen didn't like that. Apart from the physical exertion and discomfort, it had been too easy by far. The only bullets expended so far had been from the Lee-Enfields, and only on game – and the last shot had been fired over a fortnight ago.

Yes, apart from the physical exertion they'd had a pretty easy ride so far. But it didn't feel like luck. Perhaps fate was saving Jochen and his men for something special. He hoped it was a banquet.

3

In the morning, Mann was better, though still pale and shaky. Bauer was nowhere to be found.

'We'll have to send the men out to look for him,' said Jochen. 'If he's that sick he can't have gone far.'

Rudi shook his head. 'No, we can't. Bauer will just have to look out for himself. Look, I don't like it any more than you do. But he could have gone in any direction. And Siberia is really fucking *big*, Jochen. Hundreds of kilometres of trees whichever way you turn. We just don't have enough men to conduct a search.'

'But he could give us away to the Ivans.'

'What Ivans? It may have escaped your attention but there's no bugger out here except us. Besides, he left all his kit behind, so he probably intended to come back. Maybe a bear got him while he was taking a shit, or one of those tigers you were talking about. Even if he's still alive, finding him in this fucking wilderness would be a million-to-one shot. I say we bury his German bag, divvy up his food and ammo, and get moving before Hrubesch and Berger start moaning about losing time.'

'Rudi, how are you feeling this morning?'

'Me? I feel fine. Absolutely tickety-fucking-boo, as our old English teacher Friedrich Rosenbaum used to say. One of our better teachers, a really nice bloke. I wonder what happened to him?'

'He was a queer Jewish communist, Rudi. Take a wild guess.'

'Oh. Poor old Friedrich.'

Rudi was right, of course. They could search for months and never find Bauer, and if they did he'd probably be bones or bear shit. But Rudi looked as well as he claimed to be and Mann appeared to be recovering from his sickness. Jochen didn't need to worry about his friend. But Bauer's fate would just have to remain a mystery. 'Alright,' he said reluctantly. 'See to Bauer's things then give the order to strike camp and get going. I had a walk ahead early this morning and the trees are closer together, more densely packed. It's going to be tough work staying on course, especially with the mules. Hrubesch and Berger won't hear of a detour, of course. Not that I could see one.'

Rudi was silent for a moment. Then he brightened. 'Actually, that might be a blessing in disguise. If the trees are thicker, that gives us a better chance of finding nuts and berries, maybe mushrooms. Fresh food, Jochen. Think about it. When was the last time you ate something that didn't come out of a tin or a greaseproof paper packet?'

'Must be nearly two weeks ago, when Winkler shot that elk or whatever it was.'

Rudi grinned. 'Winkler thought it was a cow, the silly

sod. He must be the only Holsteiner in history who doesn't know what a fucking cow looks like.'

'To be fair, he's from Lübeck, not a farm. I was talking to him a couple of days ago. Before the war he was an accountant. Most of our men are actually city boys, just like us. Apparently, our allegedly superior officers think anyone from outside the major cities is a yokel. They'd all been on a horse before but other than that they know as much about living in the country as I do about running a circus. Wouldn't know a damson from a damselfly. Hey, that's a thought. Maybe Bauer and Mann helped themselves to those Fliegenpilz that seem to thrive around here.'

'Those red and white mushrooms? I shouldn't think so. Berger warned us about them. He reckons they can send you bonkers.'

'They can also cause vomiting and diarrhoea. The symptoms match. Perhaps Bauer ran off because he was seeing things again.'

'Yeah, but I saw things and I haven't eaten any bloody Fliegenpilz. And I haven't had the pukes or the shits, even if my guts do turn over and my arse wants to express an opinion whenever I clap eyes on Karnstein. Besides, Bauer earned himself an Iron Cross at Stalingrad, for fuck's sake, fought off a Soviet attack to cover his mates while they retreated – sorry, *regrouped* – even though he'd copped a bullet in the shoulder. He's one very tough fucker. If Zhukov's lads couldn't scare him, I can't see him running away from a poxy hallucination.'

'An Iron Cross is pretty much standard issue for this unit. We've all got one, even Karnstein. Except maybe Berger and Hrubesch.' Jochen rubbed his eyes. 'This isn't getting us anywhere, Rudi. The fact is that Bauer's gone and we can't hang around waiting for him. Let's get ready to move out.'

The dense layer of trees turned out to be no more than half a kilometre deep but it still took them the best part of six hours to thread their way through, guiding and cajoling the fractious mules. Now they faced a different challenge.

The swamp was obscured by both mist and thick swarms of midges. And the sky was much darker than it should have been, though there didn't appear to be a cloud in the sky. Jochen's wristwatch said it was just after two in the afternoon, yet the light suggested mid-evening. He peered into the mist and gloom from several angles but couldn't see further than about fifty metres ahead, or to his left or right. There was no telling how wide the swamp was, or how deep it might be.

'We must press on,' said Hrubesch. Berger, with evident reluctance, nodded agreement.

'Well, we can't make camp here,' said Rudi. 'The midges are bad enough but there are mosquitoes as big as fucking Stukas. I'm being eaten alive. Mind you, I don't much fancy wading through that bastard lot. It looks like shit and it stinks even worse.'

Hrubesch narrowed his eyes and pursed his lips as he always did when he heard swearing. Again, Jochen questioned whether the man belonged to the Ahnenerbe. He acted more like a prissy backwater priest than a man of science, no matter how exotic his field of study might be. Rudi, of course, had noticed Hrubesch's sensitivity to foul language and cranked it up whenever the latter was within earshot. Berger, in stark contrast, didn't give a damn about anything but the mission and, unlike his sour-faced colleague, was even willing to muck in with setting up and striking camp. And occasionally, he was even prepared to make constructive suggestions.

'Rub mud on your face, neck and hands,' said Berger. 'It will keep the insects off.'

'It'll keep the ladies away too,' said Rudi gloomily. 'Not that there any out here.'

'Just think of the fun you'll have catching up when we return to the Fatherland,' Berger replied. 'You'll be a hero all over again. Women will be queuing up to warm your bed.'

'Wading through that horrible shit doesn't strike me as being fucking heroic,' Rudi griped. 'It'll take months to wash that bastard stench off. I'll have to look for girls with chronic anosmia.' He slapped at a mosquito that had settled on his cheek, then inspected the remains. 'Fuck a duck, these bastards are gigantic. Why couldn't they have given us a bloody Flak instead of a sodding flag?'

Hrubesch and Berger wandered back into the trees, conversing quietly. Jochen wondered what they were talking about. Berger seemed animated, Hrubesch impassive. They were chalk and cheese, those two – Berger nearly two metres tall, brown-haired and thin as a rake, Hrubesch a head shorter, blond and stocky. One more or less friendly and sociable; the other aloof, cold and prudish. This wasn't the first time Jochen had seen them arguing quietly, though he'd never been made privy to their disagreements. On the other hand, scientists did seem to make a point of dispute.

Rudi was still eyeing the swamp with a combination of

suspicion and horror. 'There could be anything lurking in there. Sharks, crocodiles... Hippos, even.'

Jochen took pity on him. 'I'll go first,' he said. 'I'll cut a long branch and use it to test the depth as we go along. If it gets too bad we'll come back and try to find a way round, and to hell with Hrubesch. What are you grinning about?'

'Oh, I'm just thinking that Karnstein is about ten centimetres taller than me, and he's got a head on him like a prize pumpkin. Just think how many mosquitoes will be able to feast on that big bastard.'

Jochen laughed. 'I know Karnstein is a bit of a prick, but why do you dislike him so much? I know you think he's an SD spy, but your dislike seems personal.'

Rudi became serious. 'I've heard him boasting. About what he did to Jews in Poland and Gypsies in the Ukraine. He's a fucking butcher, Jochen, a beast worse than any animal. And the other Sturmmänner, they just fucking lap it up. They've all got Jew and commie stories to tell – torture and maiming, rape and beating and killing. These men were handpicked for this mission, Jochen – hard cases, fanatical Nazis, true fucking believers prepared to do the worst possible things in the name of the Reich and Aryan purity. They're psychos, mate, really fucking dangerous nutters. Himmler wanted men who would be willing to do *anything* to complete this mission.'

'Then why pick me to lead it? Why allow me to choose you as my second?'

Rudi sighed. 'Because of what we told them about what happened in the Ukraine. What they think we did. Himmler believes we're like the others, that's why. Shit, *history* will see us as men like them. If the Allies win this war, we'll be well and truly fucked. If we survive, that is, which at this moment seems increasingly unlikely.'

'Well, we are soldiers in wartime. It's not exactly a risk-free job.'

'That's not what I mean. Karnstein has his eye on you, and I know for a fact he's been whispering to the others about us. Insinuating that we're queer, that we lack full commitment to the cause, snide shit like that. He may only be a Sturmmann, but he isn't acting like one.'

'I've seen his service record, Rudi. Despite the Iron Cross, he's been passed over for promotion several times. He may be an exceptionally loyal Nazi, but operationally he has shown poor judgement and lack of discipline. He'll never be an officer. He's here for the same reason as the others – to provide muscle.'

'Exactly. And how many of the others have any flaws at all in their records? None, that's how many. Karnstein doesn't add up. SD or not, whatever he is, he isn't Waffen-SS. All I can think is that he's here because he's a real blue-eyed boy, such a fanatic that if Himmler says this mission is of vital importance to the Reich, Karnstein will do his damnedest to make sure it succeeds. That means taking us out of the picture if we show any signs of weakness or indecision. The mission comes first, everything and everyone else is expendable. And that brings me to the mission itself. Hrubesch and Berger haven't told us what it is yet, but if Himmler put together a team of utterly ruthless and vicious fanatics to pull it off, then I'm thinking it must be something very bad indeed. And what the fuck could be out here in the middle of Siberia that's so important? And why did we bring that box?'

'Box? What are you talking about?'

'Well, you know Hrubesch gave strict instructions that we were not, under any circumstances, to look at those big packages the mules are carrying?'

Jochen groaned. 'You looked, didn't you?'

'Of course I fucking did. My dad may have been a useless, drunken waste of space with the brains of a turd, but Frau Brandt didn't raise her only son to enjoy ignorance, Jochen. Anyway, the mule packs include a disassembled radio set, a few carpentry tools, and a couple of uniforms – it was dark so I couldn't see what colour but they were quality tailoring – and two swords with scabbards and belts. But there were also six wooden panels, pretty sturdy, each one lined with lead sheeting, really fucking heavy, and a bag of screws and nails. I feel sorry for those poor mules, what with carting the water cans as well. Anyway, two panels have three sets of steel rings attached. Each panel has holes already drilled for screws. The dimensions, the way the holes line up – it's a rectangular, lead-lined box, the size and shape of a coffin. The parts need only to be screwed together. Now what is that for, I ask you? Are we here to steal a bleeding corpse?'

'A corpse? I shouldn't think so. Unless Himmler has got wind of some long-lost Aryan hero buried out here. More holy relics to ensure a glorious victory. But I can't think of anyone who might fit the bill. No, it can't be that.'

'Then why the fuck do we need a lead-lined box?'

'Well, coffins used to be lined with lead,' Jochen reluctantly allowed. Then he remembered another use for the metal. It didn't explain the special uniforms but it had to be the key. 'Radioactivity,' he muttered incredulously.

'That must be it. For months there have been rumours that the Reich is developing an atomic weapon, an extraordinarily powerful bomb. To be honest, I never really believed it was possible. But lead shields from radiation, Rudi. There must be a secret Soviet research facility hidden away out here. Perhaps radiation is what Hrubesch's pendulum is detecting. The mission must be to steal radioactive materials from the Ivans.'

Rudi's eyes widened. 'Bloody hell, Jochen. I'm thinking this facility will be really heavily guarded. Two old farts and seventeen of us armed with MP 40s won't be enough. They should have sent a fucking Panzer division.'

4

The birch pole sank no more than half a metre into the ooze. So far, so good. Jochen took another pace forward, tested the swamp again, with the same result. From behind came muffled curses as the Soviet midges and mosquitoes went about their business of drinking German blood, and as someone urged the mules onward.

That was his five hundredth pace, which at around fifty centimetres a step meant they'd covered around a quarter of a kilometre of swamp, though he couldn't swear they'd been travelling in a straight line, not with the mist obscuring his view in all directions. He turned to check that Rudi was still in sight. His friend grinned unconvincingly and gave him a thumbs-up.

The mist was bad enough, but the near-total silence was wholly unnerving. Nothing moved except the unit and those damnable insects. Jochen would have expected to see or hear frogs in a place like this, perhaps a rat or two, but there appeared to be none. Other than a few clumps of sickly-looking reeds, all he could see was a depressing expanse of dark brown tinted green by microscopic algae. The ooze – watery as cheap broth in places but mostly as thick as old custard – was unnervingly warm, presumably from whatever biological or chemical processes were generating the appalling smell. Overhead, the sky seemed darker than ever, though still there were no visible clouds, only a flat sheet of grey.

At the rear someone – it sounded like one of the Pfeiffers, most likely the fool with the warts on his face – started singing the *Horst Wessel Lied*, quickly curtailed by Rudi's hissed 'Shut the fuck up, you idiot.' Then he heard someone retch as the stench, impossibly, worsened. Bubbles of acrid gas, stirred up to the scummy surface by his feet, popped like overripe boils. It was like wading through a lake of rotting shit and decaying liquid flesh.

The world collapsed, shrinking until it seemed no more than a vague suggestion of a tunnel through thick, yellowish fog that deadened all sound and numbed his soul. Jochen plodded on, hawking and spitting to clear his throat and lungs of stinking mist and stray droplets of the vile mud, pausing only to wipe sweat and foul condensation from his stinging eyes with his relatively clean left hand.

This is like a scene from Dante, he thought, though he couldn't recall a circle of hell in the *Inferno* reserved exclusively for the foolhardy, and none quite like this. Perhaps this was where portmanteau sinners were consigned, those whom Satan himself was unable to categorise. Jochen didn't believe in God or the Devil, or in any system of post-mortem punishment and reward for this life's deeds – but this swamp certainly lived up to his idea of damnation. Someone should have put up iron gates and a sign. *Lasciate ogne speranza, voi ch'intrate. Arbeit macht frei.*

At last, the pole only sank to a depth of about thirty centimetres, then fifteen, until finally the slime no longer covered his boots. A few minutes later, he was walking on dry land, a twenty-metre stretch of coarse, uneven turf between swamp and yet more trees. He went to the nearest birch and collapsed, panting, revelling in the relatively clean air. Rudi sat heavily beside him. 'Fucking hell,' he gasped. 'I always knew that one day I'd be up Shit Creek without a paddle. But nobody told me I wouldn't have a sodding boat either.' Jochen attempted a laugh but thought better of it and delicately fished the cigarettes from his stained shirt pocket so he could have a smoke instead.

One by one, the rest of the unit followed. Jochen did a quick head-count, then another. Mules all present and correct, if understandably ill-tempered after their ordeal. But only seventeen men, plus himself. Someone else was missing.

'Well, I'm not going to look for him,' said Rudi. 'No way am I wading through that shit again. Winkler will just have to find his own way out. And Mann should have fucking checked that Winkler was still behind him.'

'Perhaps he was confused by the mist,' Berger offered. 'Or he fell and was unable to get up again.'

Hrubesch was less sympathetic. 'Or perhaps he and Bauer simply deserted. A little hardship was too much for them.'

'No way,' said Rudi vehemently. 'You're talking about loyal men, Hrubesch. Men who, whatever any other faults they may have, are not fucking cowards. Tough men, used to roughing it and facing danger. Not deserters. Something must have happened to them.'

'And what might that be?' There was a hint of a sneer in Hrubesch's voice. 'You would do well to remember your rank, Obersturmführer. Wild talk like that could undermine morale and put the mission at risk.'

Rudi bristled. 'Fuck you, Hrubesch. I'm simply stating facts. Men like Bauer and Winkler do not run away when the going gets a bit sticky.'

'Gentlemen,' said Berger, raising his hands. 'Bickering will solve nothing. Two men have gone and we must accept that something, as the Obersturmführer said, must have happened to them. Volitional or otherwise, we do not yet know. However, the mission must proceed with or without them. Hauptsturmführer?'

Jochen lit another Eckstein and roused himself from sudden torpor. 'Yes, naturally. Obersturmführer Brandt, I know you're upset about losing another man, but please show some respect.'

Rudi exhaled and rubbed at the dried mud on his forehead. 'Of course. That was uncalled for, and I'm sorry. These mosquito bites are itching like fuck and it's making me cranky. That and the bloody God-awful smell. Not to mention the chafing. Perhaps we should move further into the trees and set up camp for the night. Everyone's worn out. Nothing boosts morale like sleep and food, right? Except women and beer, that is. Christ, what wouldn't I give for a beer right now.'

'We cannot rest yet,' said Hrubesch. 'We must go on while we still have daylight.'

'No,' said Jochen flatly. 'I fully appreciate the importance of the mission, but the Obersturmführer is correct. The mission will not succeed if the men are too exhausted to fight effectively or too demoralised to think clearly. A bit of extra sleep will do us all the world of good. We'll stop for the night at the next passable open space.'

Hrubesch opened his mouth to protest but Berger unexpectedly stepped in again. 'I agree with the Hauptsturmführer. We're going to need our wits about us in the coming days. And believe me, the mission will require all our strength. We need every man fit and healthy. That includes you and me, Wilhelm. And I for one am just about ready to drop. The doctor prescribes an early night.'

Hrubesch nodded reluctantly. 'Of course, Heinz. I bow to your greater expertise.'

Jochen looked from Berger to Hrubesch and back. Something had passed between the two but he was damned if he could guess what it was.

Everyone was sick. The night had passed without incident but in the early morning light it was clear that the entire unit had been struck down by the same illness that had affected Bauer and Mann a few days previously.

'It's that fucking swamp,' Rudi moaned after yet another visit to the trees to empty his bowels. 'Those bastard mosquitoes have given us malaria.'

'No one is shivering,' Jochen pointed out. He'd just thrown up again and his throat was thick with bitter slime. 'So I'm fairly certain it isn't malaria. But you're probably right about the swamp. We probably ingested bacteria while we were crossing. God knows I swallowed enough of that vile muck. Couldn't help it. And I daresay not being able to wash it off hasn't helped. Strange thing is, I don't feel properly ill, if you know what I mean. It's more like a weird feeling of dread that's upsetting my digestive system. You know, like when you're a kid and you do something to get in trouble – that queasy feeling when you know you're going to be punished with more than a finger-wagging and a slap on the wrist. Only fifty times worse.'

Rudi nodded. 'Well, I didn't like to say. But yes, I know what you mean. Jochen, I feel really fucking scared and I don't know why.'

Jochen stood and swayed, immediately dizzy. 'One thing's for sure. We won't be going anywhere today. Hopefully this will pass fairly quickly.'

'Hrubesch won't like that.'

'Hrubesch is as sick as the rest of us. Only the mules seem well, though they're a bit more skittish than usual today. Take it from me, we've got the day off. Not that we'll be able to enjoy it.' Jochen turned his head away and vomited into the fire, which hissed and crackled noisily. 'God, that was disgusting,' he said hoarsely, wiping his mouth on his sleeve. 'You know, I've been trying to do a head count all morning but everyone's running in and out of the trees so much I can't keep tabs on them. At one point I got up to twenty-seven before giving up.'

'Don't worry, I did it myself before you got up, when I could still walk more than two fucking metres without shitting my pants. Eighteen. We're all here that's going to be. It's a shame, really. I was hoping Karnstein would fuck off like Bauer and Winkler.'

Jochen pulled a face. 'Let's hope not. I have a feeling

we might need a man like him before we're done.'

Rudi was shocked. 'Jochen, we'll *never* need a man like Karnstein. And if we ever did, what would that make us?'

'True Schutzstaffel officers, that's what.' Jochen closed his eyes. 'God, that's a depressing thought. You know, when we were given this mission I hoped it would get us away from all that SS nonsense. A few weeks away from the war, a little while longer of avoiding being assigned to the concentration camps or sent back to the Eastern Front, a break from having to pretend to be obedient little Nazis around our fellow officers.'

'Well, we'll have to get back to all that Aryan superman bollocks sooner or later. If we make it.'

'I don't think I can do it anymore, Rudi. We're in bed with evil, you know, and sooner or later it's going to tell us to turn over and think of the Fatherland. I think I want to defect.'

Rudi laughed. 'To the Allies? That's crazy talk. At best they'd put us in a prison camp. At worst?' He shrugged. 'You know damned well the Ivans would shoot us on sight. The British and Americans would interrogate us until we bled, then lock us up and throw away the key until they remembered to shoot us. If they know about what we are supposed to have done in the Ukraine, they'll probably hang us. And when the war ends, if the Allies win we'll be tried for war crimes and probably strung up anyway, and if the Reich wins we'll be shot as deserters. There are no good permutations, my friend. We are screwed whichever way you look at it. All we can do is hope for the best, whatever the fuck that will turn out to be. A straight choice between frying pan and fire, no doubt.' Rudi rose unsteadily to his feet. 'Bugger this for a lark, I'm going to lie down for a little while to rebuild my strength. A month should do it.'

Watching Rudi wobble to his tent, Jochen bitterly regretted involving his friend in this bizarre and increasingly unpleasant mission. Just one more good intention cemented into the crazy-paved road to Hell. He shook his head vigorously in an effort to dispel the buzzing in his head. Actually, a contagious inner-ear infection might explain the symptoms they were all experiencing. He remembered his father vomiting and complaining of giddiness and ringing in the ears after a particularly bad cold. The doctor had diagnosed labyrinthitis and assured him the condition would be temporary. The symptoms had passed in a couple of weeks and his father had been none the worse for it. But this was different.

For one thing, the noise appeared to bypass his ears and manifest directly within Jochen's skull. For another, this was no mere ringing, hissing or buzzing. It was more of an intense internal itch, a sensation like thousands of insects crawling around inside his head, a myriad chitinous legs scraping away at his brain. The very thought made him want to vomit again. His digestive system duly obliged, a cascade of watery, bitter gastric juices extinguishing the fire completely. He crawled to his tent, covered himself with the rough blanket, and closed his eyes against his troubles.

5

'Hoffmann? Which one's he?' Jochen was feeling much better and the noise in his head had ceased. But his mind was still foggy from sleep and he desperately wanted breakfast. It was far too early in the morning for bad news.

'The really big bloke with half his left ear missing. Ugly fucker. Face like Boris Karloff with a really bad hangover. And that was before he got sick.'

'God in heaven, Rudi. Not another one. No sign of him anywhere?'

'Not a trace. He left all his stuff, just like Bauer.'

'What on earth is going on?'

'I've been thinking about that. I reckon we're being stalked by one of those tigers you were talking about. It's following us and grabbing men when they go into the trees for a shit. One every few days, when it gets hungry. Sneaky buggers, tigers. You only know they're there when it's too late. Stalk, pounce, bang – that's you fucked.'

A tiger? It made as much sense to Jochen as any other

explanation he'd heard so far. 'Surely whoever was on watch would have heard something? A scream?'

'Tigers are bloody fast, Jochen. And they kill by clamping their jaws over your face so you can't breathe, suffocate you. Or is that lions? Same difference, I suppose.'

'So we're down to seventeen men, and two of those are Hrubesch and Berger. I can't see them being any use in a fight, so that means we have a grand total of fifteen trained soldiers. We can't afford to lose anyone else. Issue instructions that no one is to leave the camp at night alone. If anyone needs to relieve himself, he takes someone to keep a lookout. If anyone complains, tell them privacy could mean death.'

'Winkler went in broad daylight,' Rudi pointed out.

'In that swamp? It might as well have been night, it was so dark in there. But the same rule applies when we're on the move, just in case. Two abreast except for whoever's taking point, which is usually me. Nobody out of visual range. Maintain vigilance at all times.'

Rudi sketched a salute. 'Shouldn't have too much trouble getting the message through. The men are beginning to get nervous. Except Karnstein, that is. Nothing bothers that arsehole. Apart from me and you.'

'And for God's sake don't mention tigers. They'll be shooting at every bloody shadow and fluttering leaf.'

When he was alone in his tent, Jochen lit a cigarette and thought long and hard about the mission, which had become a kind of slow, creeping nightmare, and it had gone on long enough. If Hrubesch and Berger didn't tell all by nightfall, he would force the issue. What he did after that would depend on what they had to say.

Late that afternoon, fortune at last smiled on them. The trees thinned and their route became a recognisable trail. Less than a metre wide, overgrown with grasses and other plants in places, still it was much easier to negotiate than weaving their way through packed birch and tangled undergrowth. It had a natural look to it, the sort of path larger animals might create over many years – deer or badgers, perhaps. Back in the countryside around Leipzig, Jochen had seen many such tracks. Some of the badger setts there, he'd been told, were centuries old, and the creatures' foraging routes had become paths followed by humans for just as long.

Even Hrubesch seemed buoyant, presumably because the easier going would help make up for time lost to the previous day's collective illness. Thinking about it, Jochen was surprised that everyone seemed so much better. The men, Rudi included, all looked a little pale and most of them had visibly lost weight. Jochen himself had cut another notch in his belt so his trousers wouldn't fall ignominiously down around his ankles. Yet he did feel rather well. He began to cheer up.

Five kilometres along the trail, they came to a large, roughly circular clearing, without trees or shrubs and maybe fifty metres in diameter. The trackway continued on the other side. Although there was no grass or small flora, the clearing was not empty. Rudi stepped up beside him, nostrils twitching. 'What's that smell? It's… Well, it's *nice*.'

'Sage,' said Berger, who had come up behind them unnoticed. So much for maintaining vigilance. 'Someone's been here and planted a sage lawn. Interesting.' His face lit up. 'But not as interesting as those.' He pointed across the clearing to where the trail went on. Two roughly rectangular stone objects, about two and a half metres tall and half that in width, stood either side of the path. Berger strode rapidly toward them, flanked by Jochen and Rudi. Behind them, Hrubesch and Karnstein appeared, following like malevolent shadows.

Jochen peered at the slabs. Each was carved with an impression of human features – nose, mouth and eyes; nipples; a line separating the lower half vertically, indicating legs; an arm high across the breast; a belt from which hung a doubled axe and a dagger. Their bellies just above the belts were carved with ornate animals. 'What are they?'

'Archaeological treasure,' said Berger excitedly. 'I've seen objects like this before, when I was in the Ukraine, in 1927. They're Bronze Age stelae – upright stone slabs – made by Aryan nomads, the people we call Scythians. Similar carved slabs, called deer stones, are common across Siberia, and were still being erected well into the Middle Ages by Turkic tribes, obviously in imitation of the Aryans who preceded them. The axes and daggers on these, however, are typical of Bronze Age implements in Europe. And pronouncedly anthropomorphic features like this are very rare outside the Ukraine, though they have much in common with certain engravings in elsewhere in Europe, Central Asia and Anatolia. You see those carvings on their abdomens? The postures and well-defined musculature suggest power and speed. Superbly executed. Mind you, those knots like curved teardrops at the leg joints look more Celtic or Pictish than anything else. These are definitely ancient Aryan artefacts and utterly unique in my experience.

I must prepare my camera!'

'That one looks like a skinny wolf,' said Rudi. 'Or a dog. And what's that one? A cat?'

'A lynx,' said Berger confidently. 'Look at the short tail and tufted ears, the stippled spots. A Eurasian lynx. Quite remarkable.'

Rudi was unimpressed. 'What do they mean?'

'Nobody knows. The human features could represent gods, heroes, ancestors, kings. The stones could be territorial totems, boundary markers. But in the ancient world feline and canine images were frequently displayed to ward off evil spirits, suggesting their true function may be apotropaic.'

Rudi exchanged a mystified glance with Jochen. 'Apple-what?'

'Apotropaic. Magical protection, Obersturmführer.'

Jochen cleared his throat. 'What exactly is your field of expertise, Berger? Hell, I don't even know your title. Do I call you "doctor" or "professor" or just plain "mister"?'

'Whichever you prefer. All are applicable. I used to be a professor of archaeology at Heidelberg, with an interest in folklore and mythology. I also studied medicine for a while. Then I gave up that life to join the – ah, the…'

'Let's just say we combine our academic and technical expertise with patriotic duty,' Hrubesch interrupted smoothly.

'You're not with the Ahnenerbe,' said Jochen. 'Are you Hrubesch?'

'We are closely affiliated. That's all you need to know for now.'

Berger tugged at Hrubesch's elbow. 'We must camp

here tonight, Wilhelm. I want to sketch those stelae while we still have light.'

'Very well. While you're doing that – which is, I suppose, adding another piece to the jigsaw puzzle of our great Aryan forebears – I shall consult the pendulum.'

Hrubesch walked away and dumped his pack and bags on the ground then began erecting the tent he and Berger shared. Berger produced a sketch pad from his satchel and began to draw.

'I like this sage,' said Rudi, flexing his knees and ankles. 'It's like walking on a soft rubber mat. I expect it'll be lovely to kip on.'

'Sage is a plant with magical properties,' said Berger. '*Salvia* species occur across the Northern Hemisphere and in South America. Some are used in cooking, of course, but others have different uses. American Indians burn sage because the smoke is considered purifying and believed to drive away evil spirits. One American species, *Salvia divinorum*, is said to induce mystical visions. In fact, the name *Salvia* is derived from a Latin word signifying health, well-being and healing. In this context the stelae are most definitely symbols of protection. This clearing is a place of spiritual safety and has been for a very long time. I'm sure that if you dug up a section of the sage you would find a rather deep mass of roots and old stalks, no doubt compressed by the feet of countless animals and at least a few human beings. Grazing animals would keep the sage short at the same time as stimulating new growth.'

'But there aren't any animals round here,' Jochen pointed out. 'Only our mules, and they don't count.'

Berger stopped sketching and turned to face him, his

expression indecipherable. 'Yes, that is rather worrying, isn't it? But I think we'll be perfectly safe here. For tonight, at any rate.'

Jochen watched as Berger returned to his sketch. He would, as he'd planned, double the watch throughout the night. Safety was a relative concept. Magic symbols might keep imaginary incorporeal terrors at bay, but only bullets applied to real physical threats. And just in case Rudi's man-eating tiger was a reality, he would order the men to have their MP 40s close to hand.

The campfires seemed more than usually cheering. Where they burned, the smoke billowed, augmented with the aroma of fresh sage. The smell was gorgeous and admittedly calming, though it made Jochen hungry for decent food. His yearning wasn't helped by the fact that the unit was alarmingly low on tinned food and biscuit. If they didn't find game or edible plants in the next couple of days they would be in serious trouble. The big problem with tinned rations was that once a tin was opened it had to be eaten. You couldn't carry half-empty opened cans if you were on the move. From tomorrow, they would have to share – one tin between two men, with a couple of stale biscuits, at every mealtime. It was effectively putting the men on half rations, and that was good for neither morale nor efficiency. In combat a hungry man is as prone to error as a tired one. It would make him unpopular, that much was certain. But it couldn't be helped. It was that or they would begin to starve sooner rather than later. Better to be unpopular now than face the prospect of leading a group of starved, distracted men into battle in a week's time.

With any luck, it wouldn't come to that. But the way the mission was unfolding, he couldn't rule it out. On impulse he picked a few sprigs of sage from the lawn and added them to the tin of preserved meat warming over the fire. Then Rudi sat beside him, holding out a handful of yellowish objects. 'Here, take half of these and add them to your tin of reconstituted dog vomit.'

Jochen took one, sniffed it and examined it closely. 'Fungus?'

'Pfifferlinge. What the French call chanterelles. My mum used to take me out picking mushrooms when my dad was out of work, which means quite often. You know how he was with the drink. We practically lived on mushrooms in the autumn. I got to know which ones were edible and how to tell them apart from the poisonous ones that looked similar. There are loads of in the trees just behind those statue things.'

Jochen frowned. 'You went on your own?'

'No, Berger was with me. You know, he's not a bad bloke for an Ahnenerbe egghead. A lot easier to get along with than that miserable, stuck-up git Hrubesch, that's for sure.'

'They're not Ahnenerbe, Rudi.'

'Whatever. Anyway, he asked me to tell you that him and Hrubesch want a word with you later, when the men have settled down for the night. Third watch, eleven to midnight. We can give a couple of the guys a nice break from sentry duty, Jochen. It might make them feel more kindly toward you when you cut their rations.'

Jochen was aghast. 'How the hell did you know about that? I've only just decided.'

'Don't worry, I'm not a mind-reader,' Rudi chuckled. 'I knew you'd do that because it's what I would do. It's the sensible course of action. We've got fuck-all left, mate. We could eat a mule or two, but they're sacrosanct, vital to the fucking mission. However, I suggest that before we set off tomorrow you get the men to redistribute the food so a couple of them have empty rucksacks – which I will proceed to fill with these tasty mushrooms and a fair old bit of this sage. It will supplement what we have left quite nicely. Full bellies, nutrition, and a joy to the palate. That should earn you some goodwill, as will the two or three men you gift with a lighter load. These things matter, Jochen. You're a good leader but you don't pay enough attention to the creature comforts, those little touches that mean the difference between being good and being *liked*. At the very least it might make a few of them think twice before shooting you like a fucking dog when they mutiny.'

'Mutiny? You think it will come to that?'

Rudi became serious. 'I'm sure it's already coming to it. Karnstein's been sounding out the others again, telling them you're jeopardising the mission. The usual shit – you and me are more than just good friends, he's heard you're part-Jew, that we're cowards who'd do anything to save our own skins. You know how it goes. Innuendo becomes more believable when it's whispered, Jochen. The stupid fuckers don't even get that it's you who's trying to keep them alive, while Hrubesch and Berger – decent man though he is – are leading them into what is sure to become a total fucking waste of time. They'll follow the Ahnenerbe men, maybe even Karnstein; but if they think we're untrustworthy, that means we're expendable.'

'So what do we do?'

'Well, like I said, the little things that make life more bearable, that establish your credentials as a leader who's also a decent bloke. And if I can get Karnstein on his own I'm going to take the bastard out.'

'That's murder, Rudi.' Jochen was horrified. 'They'll put you in front of a court martial. You'll be shot.'

'No, I won't,' said Rudi calmly. 'We've already had three men disappear in mysterious circumstances. A fourth will just be part of an existing pattern. It'll be easy because Karnstein will deliberately disobey your orders and go for a dump on his own. I know he will because that's the sort of man he is. By flouting your orders he'll think he's got one over on you, even if you don't know about it.'

'It's too dangerous. Someone will hear the shot.'

Rudi looked amazed. 'Jesus Christ, Jochen – have you never heard of knives? All I have to do is creep up behind Karnstein and stick the bastard spook. Slit his throat, like we were taught in training.'

'We don't actually know he's SD, Rudi. Not every swivel-eyed fanatic is a member of the cloak and dagger brigade. In any case, he could just as easily be Abwehr or Gestapo. Christ, so could any of the others. You know, I wouldn't be at all surprised to discover that every single German adult belongs to one or other of the intelligence services. Everyone spying on everyone else.'

'He's not right,' said Rudi obstinately. 'Karnstein is fucking bad news, I'm telling you.'

'Look, I trust your judgement. I agree probably is dangerous but you can't go around cutting people's throats while they're having a crap just because they *might* do something bad to you. Besides, if he's turned the Sturmmänner against us, taking out Karnstein still leaves us with more than a dozen other men to deal with. What happens then?'

Rudi stared into the fire. 'Then it's the Ukraine all over again.'

'I'd rather not go down that road, but if that's what it takes then I don't see what choice we have. We may have no alternative.'

'Well, we could just bugger off and leave them to it. Travel light, just the two of us, move fast. Head due south to the Trans Siberian Railway, follow it west to where we left the horses, retrace our steps to Manchuria, slip past the Ivans and the Japanese, fuck off to unoccupied China, see out the rest of the war in some remote little village. Eat rice and noodles and chicken in sweet and sour sauce. Shit, do you remember those Chinese restaurants that time we went to Hamburg? Heaven on a tablecloth. Chicken chow mein. Pork balls with sweet and sour sauce. Christ, I could kill for a plate of crispy duck Karnstein, given a choice.'

'Will you stop going on about Karnstein for five bloody minutes? Anyway, that Chinese food may be damned good but right now I'd much rather have cakes, good old belly-filling German stodge. Schneckennudeln or Franzbrötchen, or Bratapfel. Anything with cinnamon. I absolutely love cinnamon.' Jochen consulted his scratched and dented Stowa wristwatch. 'Right, it's nearly eleven. Let's go and see what Hrubesch and Berger have to say.'

6

Hrubesch and Berger were waiting by the Scythian stelae. So too was Karnstein. Rudi glared at his *bête noir*. 'What the fuck is *he* doing here?'

Karnstein returned the glare, with a sneer attached. 'What the fuck are *you* doing here?'

'Obersturmführer Brandt is my second-in-command,' said Jochen levelly. 'If anything happens to me he will be in charge of the mission's security. Therefore, he must be kept informed of all developments.'

'He doesn't need to know this,' said Karnstein. 'My orders are quite clear. Only you and I are to be told, no one else.'

'What rank do you hold in the SD, Karnstein? Or is the Gestapo?'

'It's the Abwehr, actually.' Karnstein smiled at Jochen's shocked expression. 'Military intelligence,' he added, as though further clarification was necessary. 'I'm an Oberleutnant, not a Sturmmann. I was attached to this mission on instructions from Reichsmarschall Göring, at the request of Reichsführer Himmler. My function is to advise as required, provide additional oversight, and give you the benefit of my specialist skills. Also, it was felt the mission would benefit from closer co-operation between the SS and the Wehrmacht. Especially considering the extreme overzealousness so often displayed by SS units.'

Jochen raised his eyebrows as he decoded that. *Well, isn't that just brilliant – even Himmler doesn't trust the SS to pull this off without getting heavy-handed and maybe damaging whatever we're here to find.* 'So your SS service record is a fabrication?'

Karnstein shrugged. 'That's my legend, my cover story. Standard procedure for undercover intelligence operatives. Some of it's genuine – the cartographical background and the Iron Cross. But the rest is not at all relevant to this discussion. My orders, however, *are* relevant.'

Jochen thought for a moment. 'If memory serves, and unless there has been a recent change of which I am wholly unaware, an Oberleutnant is directly equivalent to an Obersturmführer. Correct?'

Another shrug. 'Correct.'

'Then I outrank you. And as Hrubesch and Berger here are in charge of the technical aspects of this mission, and I am in charge of the actual operation and the Sturmmänner assigned to the mission – and you are, on paper at least, one of them – I order you to *shut the fuck up*. Obersturmführer Brandt stays, and that is that. Now then, I believe Hrubesch and Berger have something to tell us.'

Karnstein opened his mouth to protest. Jochen drew the Luger from his waistband and aimed at Karnstein's face. 'Unless you really, *really* want me to shoot your ugly nose off, the only words I want to hear from you until I am enlightened to my satisfaction by Berger and Hrubesch are "Permission to speak, Hauptsturmführer" – understood?'

Karnstein's eyes blazed but he nodded weakly. Jochen turned to Hrubesch and Berger, who were staring at him with round eyes. 'Gentlemen, you have the floor.'

Hrubesch cleared his throat. 'You may find some of this hard to believe…' He paused, seemingly uncertain of how to begin.

Berger took up the slack. 'Actually, you'll find *all* of it hard to believe. Perhaps impossible. You will need to suspend that disbelief, just for a few minutes. The story begins with a coincidence: stories told by refugees and a smuggled document. They came to the attention of Hans Vögel, a specialist in Aryan myth and folklore, an esteemed colleague. Vögel notified Karl Haushofer, who immediately instructed Wilhelm and me to investigate. We pieced the rest together and informed Haushofer, who conceived this mission, with Reichsführer Himmler's approval and support.'

Rudi gasped. 'Haushofer? Fuck me, you're from the Vril Society, aren't you? Shit, and I always thought the rumours were bollocks.'

Berger nodded. 'The Vril Society is quite real, though it does not advertise its existence; and we are indeed members. We also advise the Ahnenerbe and, of course, Reichsführer Himmler. Now please, listen carefully. Our lives and the success of this mission will depend on you fully understanding what we are here to obtain. In turn, this could help determine the outcome of the war. As you know, our early victories and territorial gains are crumbling away, largely because of American intervention forcing us to wage war on two fronts. The tide is turning against us and it is imperative that we reverse that trend. More than the Reich is at stake. While work is proceeding with new weapons that may stave off defeat and save the Fatherland from annihilation and subjugation, we are on a quest for something that could give us total victory, *global* victory; something utterly astonishing that could also transform the future of the Aryan race and cement our destiny – *forever*. Do you understand? Not a Thousand Year Reich but an *Eternal* Reich. Wilhelm? Please continue.'

It began, said Hrubesch, with stories told by ethnic Germans fleeing the Balkans. Serbian and Croat partisans were becoming prone to strange, convulsive attacks which impelled them to kill, mutilate and torture Germans – and to drink their blood. These attacks, which could be brought on by even unwitting proximity to a German, began with a hideous physical transformation – those affected would writhe and contort, foam at the mouth, shout and scream obscenities, and demand German blood to drink. Their eyes became swollen and bloodshot, and they would behave like ravening beasts, filled with rage and aggression, and temporarily endowed with superhuman strength. Some accounts even told of Serbs turning wholly into animalistic creatures that were no longer human. The worst were those partisans who hid in the Yugoslav forests, and their bloodthirsty madness was allegedly encouraged by Tito. There were instances of Germans too becoming infected by the contagion. Hundreds of such reports had been received, dozens of refugees interviewed.

Hans Vögel, a friend of both Reichsführer Himmler and Walter Greite of the Ahnenerbe's Applied Nature Studies division, was fascinated by these reports. His doctoral thesis at Heidelberg had been a study of transformation themes in Aryan myth and folklore. Vögel believed that shape-changing warriors had once existed among the ancient Aryan peoples. The old myths and legends spoke of men and women who had the ability to take on monstrous forms in battle – fighters such as the Norse berserkers and the Irish hero Cúchulainn, the werewolves in France and Germany, the *benandanti* in Italy, and so on. Vögel also thought this ability was the source of Aryan tales of gods and demigods, beings with exceptional strength and preternatural senses, and the power of physical transformation.

Vögel had no doubt that something of significance was taking place in Yugoslavia. Was it a kind of mass hysteria resulting from wartime anxiety and stress? Was it unfounded rumour or propaganda repeated as if it was fact? A genuine outbreak of bloodlust that only appeared to be vampirism? Or the expression of an ancient Aryan ability that had lain dormant for centuries as we became softened by agriculture and urban living? He could not be sure, though he did observe that the Slavs were once pure Aryans – though diluted and tainted by interbreeding with Huns, Magyars, Turks and Mongols – and that this was the very region in which the modern vampire legend began. Bram Stoker may have located Count Dracula in Transylvania, but the traditional vampires of Hungary and Romania, were not the same as those that were recorded in Yugoslavia in the eighteenth century. They were not blood-drinkers.

At Vögel's behest, Reichsführer Himmler ordered the capture of a few alleged vampires. The prisoners were taken to Auschwitz, where they were examined by Josef Mengele. After full medical examinations, followed by testing with things traditionally believed to repel vampires, such as Christian holy objects and garlic, the partisans' bodies were dissected. Mengele found nothing to indicate that the supposed vampires were anything but normal human beings, albeit of an inferior type and exhibiting clear signs of violent insanity. Mengele's conclusions, however, did not mean there were no vampires or shape-changers among the partisans, only that none had yet been apprehended.

Then similar reports began to emerge from the Eastern Front. No direct witnesses could be found; and each story, reportedly heard from a friend of a friend, proved ultimately untraceable to its origin. However, at a time when the Reich's struggle against communism was precariously balanced, the tales were at best potentially demoralising. Vögel persuaded Reichsführer Himmler to instruct our intelligence operatives inside the Soviet Union to be aware of any enemy activities that might be pertinent to the phenomenon. Consequently, Vögel was given a set of curious documents obtained by an agent of the Reich operating in the Soviet Union. This dossier detailed the efforts of VIEM, the All Union Institute of Experimental Medicine, to capture a certain creature they thought might be located somewhere in the Siberian taiga.

VIEM was a secret research facility concerned with the study of toxins, drugs, hypnosis, and other methods for affecting or altering the human brain and its functions – and had an interest in shamanism and the occult. It was originally created in 1925 by the obscure 'Special Section' of OGPU, the Soviet equivalent of the Gestapo, and became a separate institution in 1934. It was similar in many ways to the Ahnenerbe.

The VIEM dossier was codenamed Baba Yaga. The first part consisted of a document dated 23rd November 1906. This was a sworn statement obtained by Alexandre Gerasimov, head of the St Petersburg branch of the Tsarist secret police, the Okhrana, from Grigori Rasputin, the notorious 'Mad Monk' who came to dominate the imperial court, and who was assassinated in the December of 1916. Rasputin had heard stories of a terrifying creature that roamed the Siberian forests, a creature that appeared to be beautiful fair-haired woman with bright blue eyes but which could change into a demonic form whose mere presence was so appalling it paralysed men with terror. The creature killed and ate people, and tortured those who tried to resist. Rasputin claimed this was the Baba Yaga of Russian folklore. But according to the monk, the old stories did not reflect the reality. He said it was in league with the enemies of Russia. The reason he came to Gerasimov was that he wanted troops to be sent to Siberia to destroy Baba Yaga. Gerasimov did not believe a word of it, merely observing that Rasputin was excitable and confused, and appeared to be drunk. No action was taken until Rasputin's testimony was discovered by VIEM.

The next document was a memo from January 1928, listing nearly forty reports of brutal killings in Siberia in the previous November and December, in an area several hundred kilometres north of Krasnoyarsk. The victims were all Communist party apparatchiks, Red Army soldiers and

NKVD spies. The memo compares these reports to Rasputin's statement. The author suggests that this supposed Baba Yaga was an indigenous shaman or sorceress with the ability to manipulate people's perceptions with her mind alone. Consequently, VIEM sent five of their specialists and a sizeable military escort to the Krasnoyarsk *oblast* where the killings took place. Not one of the sixty-one men returned, and a search party found no trace of them. That was the end of the Baba Yaga project.

Hans Vögel was fascinated by the alleged Baba Yaga's blonde hair and blue eyes, her apparent hatred of Bolshevism. He became convinced that she was not mere folklore or legend but a real being, living proof of a phenomenon of the utmost importance. This, he believed, was the Reich's opportunity to acquire an Aryan of true ancient stock, a woman with superhuman powers who could be both a weapon and potential breeding material. However, Reichsführer Himmler was busy with important matters of state and was unable to devote his attention to Vögel's suggested expedition. When the Reichsführer was able to do so, he instructed Vögel to share the VIEM documents with Karl Haushofer and the Vril Society. As a result, the Schutzstaffel and Ahnenerbe collaborated with them to set up the present mission.

Jochen was confused. Hrubesch and Berger were gazing at him expectantly. Evidently some kind of response was required. 'Let me get this straight. We're here to raid this VIEM laboratory, right? Grab what research we can and destroy what we can't, eh?'

The Vril Society men seemed disappointed by his

queations. Beside him, Rudi started to laugh. 'Oh, I don't fucking believe it,' he spluttered. 'No, Jochen – they sent us here to find this Baba Yaga thing. They want us to catch a fucking *vampire* and take it back to Germany.' He started laughing again.

'It is no laughing matter,' Hrubesch snapped. 'The future of the Reich – of our Aryan race – may depend on this.'

Rudi laughed even harder. Karnstein stepped toward him, stony-faced. Jochen raised the Luger. 'Watch yourself, Karnstein. Touch him and you're a dead man.' He turned to Berger, pointedly ignoring Hrubesch. 'What do you plan to do with this creature, if it exists?'

'First, persuade her to fight with us against the Soviets. Second, if the legends have any truth she may be able to share her abilities with an elite body of soldiers. Our scientists will study her physiology and attempt to replicate it in others.'

'You want to turn German soldiers into vampires?'

'Not necessarily,' said Berger. 'The thinking is that there may be a way to instil similar strength, speed and aggression without the less desirable traits. But, failing that…' He shrugged. 'These are desperate times that require desperate measures.'

Rudi laughed again, this time without mirth, only bitterness. 'All this way,' he growled. 'All this *fucking* way, men lost, for a fantasy. You're fucking crazy. And even if it is real, what do you expect to find? Dracula? Count Orlok?'

'Shut up, Rudi,' said Jochen. 'Berger, do you really believe this rubbish?'

'I am only obeying orders,' Berger replied, his face as

blankly pugnacious as an Arno Breker sculpture.

'Hrubesch? What do *you* think?'

'I believe there is a woman here who could transform our knowledge of the Aryan race, who is potentially a decisive weapon. Hans Vögel is a great man, a genius with profound knowledge of Aryan culture and history. If he believes, then so do I. In any case, as Heinz just said, we have our orders. We must take this woman, dead or alive.'

'Technically, that's dead or undead,' Rudi drily observed. 'And that's why you've packed a fucking coffin, isn't it? Doesn't matter what state the blood-sucking bitch is in. If she doesn't have a stake through her heart you just give her some of our claret to keep her going until we get back to Ahnenerbe headquarters. That's what we're here for – muscle to complete the mission and packed lunches for your imaginary Baba fucking Yaga on the journey home. You mad bastard fuckers. We should shoot all fucking three of you and piss off home right now.'

'Shut up, Rudi,' said Jochen again. 'Hrubesch, this is a stealth mission behind enemy lines. Why did we bring those useless uniforms?'

Hrubesch smiled. 'Our orders are to present ourselves as representatives and officers of the Reich. New uniforms for the Schutzstaffel men, special uniforms for Berger and myself, ceremonial swords. Symbols of our culture and our might, if you like.'

Jochen nodded. It made a bizarre kind of sense. 'And the radio?'

'My, you have been poking around,' said Hrubesch. 'When we complete the mission, we shall proceed to a pre-determined location and send a message to confirm completion and request extraction.'

'How will extraction be made?'

'That is not known to me. I have told you everything I know. Now you tell me, Hauptsturmführer – are you going to be an obstacle to this mission?'

Jochen saw the lie in Hrubesch's eyes. He gazed at the others. Karnstein was furious, Berger impassive, Hrubesch shrewd and calculating. Rudi's expression pleading for an end to the madness. Realistically, there was only one thing he could do.

'You're as crazy as they are,' Rudi raged. 'I cannot believe it. What the fuck has got into you?'

Jochen leaned against the stele with the lynx and lit a cigarette. The others had returned to their tents, satisfied with his response. 'Think about it, Rudi. Yes, it's a wild goose chase. There are no vampires outside books and films. Hrubesch is barking mad, Karnstein is a fanatical fuckwit who'll believe whatever he's told by his masters. I'm not sure where Berger stands. But they had an extraction plan all along. That's why they brought the radio transmitter. And I'm quite sure that plan involves code words to signal both completion and retrieval. I don't know which of them has the codes. Therefore it makes sense to go along with the mission. When we get to the location and don't find their vampire, we can go home. No harm done, except to the men we lost. Though Karnstein will probably see that we get sent back to the Eastern Front as a reward for being awkward and questioning orders.'

'Actually, that's not a bad plan,' Rudi admitted. 'Play along and get out in one piece. Pretend to be good little

Nazis for a while. At least out here they won't make us kill any Jews or beat up old ladies and little kids.'

'Not quite the Ukraine, then,' Jochen smiled.

'Fucking right it isn't,' said Rudi feelingly. 'Christ, that was a bad time. I still have nightmares about it.'

'Me too. I still don't know how we got away with it.'

'They just heard what they wanted to hear, mate. Same as Hrubesch and Berger and Karnstein. They're all caught up in their own mad dream of Germany, a fairytale Fatherland that's bigger and better and cleaner and more efficient than the real thing – one without all the poor bastards they blame for their own greed, selfishness and incompetence. Fuck knows what they'll do when all the Jews, queers, commies and cripples are gone but things still don't get any better. I suppose they'll kill everyone who deviates even slightly from the Platonic ideal of Aryan perfection, anyone who thinks even a tiny bit differently to them. In the end, there'll be just one golden-haired, blue-eyed giant Nazi left in the whole world. And when he fucks up he'll blame the animals and start on them. What a fucking mess we humans are. We're doomed.'

'It's not that bad, Rudi. Well, it might be for us as individuals – I honestly can't see an easy way out in the long term. But if the Allies win, perhaps humanity can start to make a better world.'

'Rudi snorted. 'You reckon? Do you know how many Nazi sympathisers there are in France, Britain and America? How many fascists and eugenicists and racialists and Jew-haters? Even some of the top people fighting us secretly believe in what we're doing and wish they'd had the balls to do it themselves. Mark my words, it will all start up again eventually. And as for the Ivans, they've got fucking Stalin in charge, and that mad bastard hates everyone who isn't him. So, of course, who do they all want to be like? That's the trouble with people, Jochen. They like strong leaders who think like them, which is bad news for starters, because most people are fucking idiots. And those strong leaders usually turn out to be either total lunatics or complete arseholes. Humanity couldn't make a better world in a million bastard years. We're fucked, I tell you. God in heaven, I wish I had a bottle of Korn. Two fucking bottles.'

Jochen rolled his eyes. 'Have you quite finished?' When there was no reply, he went on. 'Thank Christ for that. Ranting and raving won't help, even if it does feel good to get it off your chest. Now tell me what you know about this Vril Society. I'd never heard of it.'

'You remember that time I was assigned to the units moving the Ahnenerbe out of Berlin, after the British and Americans firebombed Hamburg?'

'Of course I remember. You didn't stop moaning about it for weeks.'

'Well, I wanted to be with the unit that took the library to Schloss Oberkirchberg, thought I might be able to nick a few interesting books. But I ended up guarding the Ahnenerbe staff moving to Waischenfeld. God, that place was a right boring old dump. Nothing to do at night except get drunk and praise the fucking Führer. I hate Bavaria. Anyway, one evening I got drunk with this physicist bloke called Wolfgang who told me a few things he probably shouldn't have, but you know me, I've got that listening kind of face, especially after a few beers. He said Himmler was really controlled by a bunch of occultists and magicians who called themselves the Thule Society, who'd dazzled him into setting up the Ahnenerbe for their benefit. But the Thule Society itself was really controlled by some people who call themselves the Vril Society, who are the ones responsible for all this Aryan bullshit. Mind you, Wolfgang wasn't entirely sure this Vril Society actually existed. Not until the sixth beer, anyway. Apparently it isn't good for your future prospects to so much as mention it. According to him, being a bigwig in the Vril Society was the only thing that kept Karl Haushofer alive – his wife is half-Jewish and Haushofer was friendly with Gregor Strasser and other left-wing Nazis who were purged from the party back in 1934.'

'So it was a rumour you heard from a drunk, while you were drunk.'

'*In vino veritas*, mate. But the Ahnenerbe is real enough, and the Thule Society seems to exist, so why not the other? It's like those Russian dolls, one bunch of smaller but nuttier nutcases inside another, until you get to the smallest and nuttiest of them all. Anyway, Wolfgang said their idea was to use the nation's resources to bring together ideas and artefacts that would help them create a purely Germanic form of magic that would enable them to channel this ancient Aryan energy called Vril. He reckoned this Vril stuff was made of particles from another dimension that sometimes intersected with ours but which usually had to be brought into our world using what we call magic, which he said is really the power of focused will.'

'You didn't tell me any of this.'

'Well, I don't tell you *everything*, Jochen. Not enough hours in the day. Besides, at the time I thought it was bollocks. Still do, actually, as far as the scientific stuff goes.

Another self-important prick telling tall tales to impress gullible people over a few drinks. But that's National Socialism at its best, folks.' Rudi yawned. 'Sod this, I'm bloody tired and I need to hit the sack. You turning in?'

'No, I'll wait here for a bit. Someone has to keep watch, remember.'

As he watched his friend shuffle off to his tent, Jochen wondered how much longer they could survive in the SS. At some point, he was sure, they would be called upon to do something truly horrific. They'd avoided it in the Ukraine, though that had been achieved at an almost equally dreadful price; but they would never be able to repeat it. Even if they made it back to Germany alive, they would in all likelihood never know peace. Their youthful ambitions were dead and would be forever denied them. Rudi's dream to be a film director would never be realised in a Reich where only propaganda was approved. A lifetime of replicating the likes of *Jud Süß* or *Die große Liebe* held no appeal for a man who idolised Murnau, Lang and Hitchcock, and who dreamed of one day seeing *Citizen Kane*. Jochen's novels would never be written, because the state wanted only anodyne patriotic entertainment and texts that either exalted the Aryan race or reaffirmed prejudices against Jews and other so-called degenerates. Schollenroman and *Der Giftpilz*, or rewriting the classics to suit Nazi ideals. Literary enslavement. So much for being the next Thomas Mann.

Nor would they be able to avoid intellectual prostitution by exchanging art for labour. The only honest jobs they would be able to get if the war was decided in the Reich's favour would be building work or farm labour, and then they would still only be serving the Nazi machine. Was that even worth the effort of drawing breath?

Hitler and his pack of slavering, rabid hounds had driven the world into a night that had lasted five long years, and still there was no sign of a dawn. Almost exactly five years of bombs and fire, bullets and bayonets, fear and death – five years of herding the unwanted, the scapegoats, into what everyone knew were really death camps. Five long years with nothing to show for the time but pain, suffering and destruction, the longest, darkest night he could have imagined. And now this mission, this prolonged act of insanity which presaged only descent into a deeper darkness.

He dropped the cigarette butt and ground it out with his toe, drawing no pleasure at all from the wisp of smouldering sage that drifted to his nostrils. If Berger was right and there was safety in that scented clearing, between those carved slabs, Rudi's words had the greater ring of truth. There was no comfort anywhere.

7

Safety, it seemed, was a relative concept. Another of their number had vanished in the night. Schuster, one of the men entrusted with handling the mules, was nowhere to be seen when Lorenz, with whom he shared a tent, awoke from troubled dreams.

'So he was already snoring you went to sleep,' said Rudi. 'And you didn't wake up at all?'

'No, Obersturmführer,' Lorenz replied. The man was clearly shaken. 'His snoring usually wakes me two or three times a night. But I slept soundly, apart from the dreams.'

'Dreams?'

'That's right, sir. I dreamed there was something sitting on my chest, something white and heavy and…' Lorenz struggled to control his emotions. 'I couldn't breathe properly and I was unable to move. And,' he glanced nervously around and lowered his voice, 'I was really scared.'

'But it was just a dream?'

'Yes, Obersturmführer. It seemed very real but I suppose it must have been a dream. Couldn't have been anything else, could it?'

Rudi eyed Lorenz critically. The soldier was a tall, muscular and barrel-chested man. But he seemed somehow depleted, his cheekbones more pronounced, shirt collar too wide for his neck, the clothes baggier. 'Lorenz, are you alright? You look as if you've lost five kilos overnight.'

Lorenz stood to attention. 'I feel fine, Obersturmführer. Nothing wrong with me, sir.'

Nothing wrong, my arse. Those trembling hands and twitchy eyelids tell a different story. It isn't just illness that's shrunk him. He's shitting himself with fear like everyone else. 'Very well. Return to your duties. Oh, and tell Ziegler to take over from Schuster with the mules.'

Lorenz hesitated. 'Ziegler doesn't like the mules, Obersturmführer. He says they stink.'

Rudi sighed. 'None of us has had a decent wash in weeks, Lorenz. We all fucking stink. If anything the mules are a bit more fragrant than the rest of us. They definitely smell better than Karnstein. Just tell Ziegler to bloody well get over it or he'll have my hobnailed boot up his fastidious bum. Now get cracking.'

The man snapped off a straight-arm salute and scurried away. Rudi shook his head. He loathed that salute. *Impotent men with tiny, limp dicks pretending they've got big, stiff cocks that actually work.* The forbidden Sigmund Freud had surely worked that one out. It just about summed up the petty, vengeful spite of the Third Reich and the jumped-up nobodies who'd somehow become its leaders. As did this ludicrous mission. *Vampires? For fuck's sake. Maybe we should be heading to the North Pole to snatch the Weihnachtsmann. A fitting project for a nation that has turned itself into a fucking Krampus.* Rudi imagined Himmler and Goebbels with blackened faces and goat horns, prancing around with phallic bundles of birch branches, stuffing naughty children with coloured triangles stitched onto their clothes into sacks labelled *Auschwitz, Dachau* and *Ravensbrück.* Overlapping yellow wedges for the Jews, pink ones for the queers, red for the commies, others he couldn't remember. Naughty children by the thousand, taken and beaten, never to be seen again. The Weihnachtsmann looking on, stern but superficially benign, his white beard transformed into a comical little moustache. Rudi would have laughed, but the joke just wasn't funny.

As he walked toward his tent Rudi had to hold his trousers up with one hand. *Either I need another breakfast or this belt needs another notch.* He paused when he caught sight of Karnstein sneaking into the trees, presumably to relieve himself. His hand strayed to the knife sheathed at his belt. *So tempting.*

Jochen thought Karnstein had been assigned to the mission to prevent the SS from getting too heavy-handed. But to Rudi that didn't make sense. Why was he posing as an SS man? That was pointless. And whatever Himmler and Göring wanted, in practice the Abwehr had no jurisdiction over the SS. If there was a concern that one or more members of the unit were less than ideologically sound, responsibility for monitoring their behaviour and ensuring compliance would surely have fallen to the Sicherheitsdienst. The Ahnenerbe was, nominally at least, part of the SS, so working with Hrubesch and Berger – who despite belonging to the Vril Society certainly had both Ahnenerbe credentials and Himmler's approval – did not technically make the mission a joint operation. But there was no reason for Abwehr involvement. Far from it – the SD was also affiliated with the SS, and the Abwehr was its bitter rival. So why?

He shook his head and resumed the short journey to his tent. Then he stopped dead in his tracks. Military intelligence. Of course. Only the Abwehr would be likely to have an agent inside the Soviet Union. More than one – a single agent wasn't much use in wartime. And a network of agents meant safe houses, supplies, radio communication and escape routes. That was why Karnstein was along for the ride. He knew who to contact and how to arrange an extraction. That was the reason Hrubesch and Berger had kept quiet when Jochen asked them about the extraction plan. They genuinely couldn't tell him about that – because they weren't actually in charge of it.

'Bollocks,' Rudi growled angrily. 'I can't kill the fucking creepy Abwehr bastard after all.'

Karnstein had suddenly become indispensable. He was their way out.

With the forest path now easily negotiable and the column of mules and men making good headway, Jochen grew bored. He left Rudi at the front and slowed down so that the others passed. Berger was plodding along just behind the mules, no doubt making sure that the unassembled coffin and his equipment came to no harm. Jochen fell in beside him.

'Tell me about Vril. I'm curious.'

Berger was surprised. 'I didn't take you for a man of science, Hauptsturmführer.'

'I'm not, but I'm not ignorant. I know a little about electricity and radio waves and X-rays but this Vril is new to me and I just want to know what you think we'll be dealing with.'

'Well, not Vril itself, I shouldn't think. But certainly a being imbued with it.'

'Is it dangerous, like atomic radiation?'

'All forms of energy are potentially dangerous, and all can be harnessed for our benefit. In that respect, Vril is no different. However, it is not harmful in the same way as radioactivity. It can both heal and destroy, revitalise and debilitate. Vril is the force of life itself.'

'I'd never heard of it. Is it a new discovery? Top secret weapons research?'

Berger laughed. 'Actually, it isn't a new discovery at all. Vril isn't even its only name. In 1871 the English author Edward Bulwer-Lytton published a novel called *The Coming Race*, which is about an ancient subterranean people of Aryan appearance, who have mastered the use of Vril in all its aspects. Helena Petrovna Blavatsky and Rudolf Steiner deduced that, although presented as a novel, *The Coming Race* was in actuality a message containing a cosmic truth for future generations. Bulwer-Lytton was not the first to intuit the existence and possible applications of this force. In the 1700s Franz Mesmer called it animal magnetism. In 1845 Baron Carl von Reichenbach named it Odic fluid, or Odyle. In 1920 Karl Schappeller called it Raumkraft. It is possibly the same as what the Hindus have called *prana* since ancient times, though we believe it is no coincidence that its modern discoverers were all Germans and Anglo-Saxons. Destiny has shown us its power, a power synonymous with life itself, maybe the same power that fuels the particles that make up the atom. We imagine it as a ray, like sunlight; but in all honesty we do not know if it a particle or a wave. Perhaps, like light, it is both. What we *do* know is that it resides outside our physical universe and although it frequently travels through whatever membranes keep one reality separate for another, it is the ultimate source of the spark of life, that which made biology from mere chemicals.'

'I think I follow,' said Jochen cautiously. 'And this Baba Yaga creature, this vampire or werewolf or whatever, she holds the secret to manipulating Vril? To turn it into a weapon, a ray-gun or something like that?'

'Perhaps. But our actual hypothesis is that Vril has in some way manipulated her physiology. Individuals like her are not born, Hauptsturmführer. Wilhelm is of the opinion that her molecular structure must have been altered by Vril to make her the way she is. Genes, the hereditary units that make up and dictate our physiology – discovered by Gregor Mendel, another German, and named by Wilhelm Johannsen, a Dane – are susceptible to alteration by atomic radiation, which suggests that a subtler, more directed force may be able to make less random and destructive changes. Vril, which Wilhelm believes may itself be sentient, would be the perfect means for inducing genetic alteration. Baba Yaga may, at the very least, be proof of that.'

It all sounded very scientific, though more than a little barmy. 'What are you going to do with her if we find her?'

Berger shrugged. 'First, try to persuade her to join the

Reich in its struggle against Bolshevism. If that fails, we will subdue her and return to the Reich with her as our prisoner. Mengele will study her and isolate desirable heritable traits. If possible, we will use her as initial breeding stock. But that is for the future. In the short term, the aim is to transfer her attributes to the Reich's finest physical specimens.'

'I can see one tiny little problem,' said Jochen, frowning. 'She's not going to be a push-over, is she? Baba Yaga or vampire, if she's as you think she is then taking her prisoner is going to be tough. What if we can't?'

'In the unlikely event that we can neither persuade nor subdue her, then we kill her. As Wilhelm said, acquiring her corpse is acceptable. Mengele can do wonderful things with a dead body, just as he can with a live one. The condition is immaterial. Alive is better but as long as genetic material survives, that will suffice.'

Jochen shuddered. From what he'd heard of Josef Mengele, the man was a ghoul. He and the vampire would doubtless make a charming couple. 'Is that why you brought that lead-lined coffin?'

'The lead will shield us from any harmful Vril emanations as her body decays. It is exactly the same principle as using lead to protect us from radiation. We have constructed appropriate facilities in Germany, at the Bergen-Belsen detainment complex. Following our return, Mengele will relocate there from Auschwitz to initiate the study. One idea is that we increase and concentrate the Vril she possesses – it may make her more powerful, or it might cause further physiological changes. We can study that process as it happens. Understand it, learn how to replicate and control it so we can achieve only desirable outcomes.'

'How would you do that?' Jochen was unable to decide if he was genuinely curious about the science, or if he simply wanted to see how much crazier Berger's explanations could get.

'We've built a Vril accumulator close to – well, let's call it another energy source.'

'A Vril accumulator?'

'An adaptation of a device recently invented in America by the renegade psychologist Wilhelm Reich. Although he is German, and in spite of his noble surname, Reich is a degenerate. Like the Jewish charlatan Freud, he is obsessed with sex. He believes the orgasm is the key to mental health, and that it creates a kind of beneficial energy, which he calls orgone, that can be accumulated in capacitors like electricity. Utter nonsense, of course. It is common knowledge that sexual abstinence conserves the vital fluids. Besides, Reich also says his orgone also occurs freely in nature, so his sexual explanation is quite clearly nothing but a way of allowing him to focus on his grand obsession, the orgasm. But we have determined that this orgone is the same as what we call Vril.'

'So you can make batteries with Vril?'

Berger shook his head. 'Not as such. Batteries make use of chemical reactions to generate electricity. While it is difficult to recharge batteries, it can be done by connecting them with the mains electricity supply. But all that does is refresh the chemical reactions so a battery can be used again. It does not store the electricity as such. Reich's accumulator, on the other hand, can store Vril by trapping the rays between alternating layers of organic and inorganic materials – wood and metal, for instance. That is our greatest hope. By placing the woman known as Baba Yaga in such an accumulator, we should be able to increase and concentrate the Vril in her tissues so that when a soldier of the Reich is placed inside with her, it will change him in exactly the same way. Faster, stronger and deadlier, utterly ruthless – a thousand such men will be equal to a million of our enemies' forces. And they will show no mercy.'

'What do you reckon?' asked Rudi when Jochen had returned to the front of the column.

Jochen grimaced. 'I reckon he's completely barking mad. And compared to Hrubesch, Berger's the sane one. They really do believe this Baba Yaga is real, and that we can capture it.'

'For fuck's sake. Look, I've seen *Dracula* and *Nosferatu*. Us against something like that? My money's on Bela Lugosi or Max Schreck, with or without the fucking greasepaint. We're all knackered and half-starved. A toddler could knock us over with a fart. Christ, it's just as well Hrubesch and Berger are as potty as a parade of china shops. If that thing was real...' He shuddered and looked expectantly at Jochen's cigarettes.

'Just as well it isn't, eh?' Jochen offered Rudi an Eckstein and they lit up. 'No, all we have to worry about is making sure Karnstein gets us out of here and back to Germany. Maybe we can persuade him to drop us off in a neutral country.'

'I've been thinking about the journey home. I think it'll be by plane. It's the only way – fly us across Russia to Finland, then along the Swedish coast and over to Denmark. That would avoid crossing the Eastern Front or crossing Allied lines elsewhere. Sweden's neutral. Maybe we could force Karnstein to put us down somewhere near Stockholm. Then him and the other lunatics can fuck off back to the Reich and leave us to see the war out in peace. You can write your novel and I'll make it into a film.'

'And where do we get a typewriter and movie camera? We're not carrying any money, Rudi. Himmler didn't exactly throw the Reich's coffers wide open for us to help ourselves. All we were given was that bit of gold we exchanged in Manchuria for horses and mules, these old rifles and our civilian clothing. Anyway, why should we have needed money on this trip? We're not here to go shopping.'

'I suppose you're right,' Rudi sighed. 'In any case, Hitler's already taken Denmark and Norway. Neutral or not, it's only a matter of time before the Reich annexes Sweden. Then where would we go?'

The conversation came to an abrupt end when Rudi stumbled to a halt and pointed a trembling finger at what lay directly in their path. 'What the fuck is *that*?'

8

Bauer, Winkler, Hoffmann and Schuster gazed up at them from empty eyes sockets. Four severed heads, in varying stages of decay, lay in a neat line across the trail, each with its own halo of flies.

Rudi cleared his throat. 'I'm thinking it's definitely not a tiger that's done that,' he said.

Jochen's face was grim. 'They've been a bit, well, chewed. That bite on Hoffman's cheek – it looks human.'

The remaining colour fled from Rudi's face. 'Cannibals?' He stared wildly around.

'Just over ten years ago parts of the Soviet Union were hit by a major famine caused by Stalin's crazy agricultural policies. One of those Ukrainian recruits told me millions died of starvation in the Ukraine alone. He called it the Holodomor, which apparently means "murder by starvation" in Ukrainian. It wasn't just the Ukraine, though. Cannibalism was rife all across the Soviet Union, people even eating their kids so nobody else would eat them. Body parts sold in street markets. Perhaps someone acquired a taste for human flesh.'

'But not the heads, it seems,' said Rudi pensively.

'Maybe it's a religious thing. Siberia has even more weird cults than America. They're bound to have some bunch of maniacs who will eat human bodies but treat the head as a sacred object.'

'Shit, what shall we do with them?'

'We'll have to move them aside.'

'Fuck that,' said Rudi. 'I'm not touching them. They're all rotten and maggoty. And there's something living in Bauer's nose.'

'Then just kick them out of the way.'

Rudi was horrified. 'But that's disrespectful. How would you like it if I did that to your head?'

'I'd be dead and wouldn't care a damn,' Jochen told him.

'I think we should tell Berger and Hrubesch about this right away. And Karnstein.'

'Karnstein? Why him?'

Rudi grinned nastily. 'Someone's got to shift those heads. I can't wait to see the look on his face.'

Hrubesch and Berger declined to visit the grisly scene. But Karnstein surprised them. He stared sombrely down at the heads for a moment. Without a word, he carefully gathered them into his arms and laid them gently at the base of a tree. He stood over them, at attention, eyes closed and lips moving soundlessly, then silently and reverently covered them with ferns and strips of moss.

'They died for the Fatherland,' said Karnstein. 'They died as soldiers. We shall honour them by completing this mission.'

Jochen nodded. 'Let's hope the mission honours them by being worth their lives.'

Karnstein seemed puzzled. 'It most certainly shall be, Hauptsturmführer. Who do you think did that to them? It was Baba Yaga's work.' He turned on his heel and made his way to the rear of the column.

'Great,' said Rudi. 'That's just what we need. Another fucking true believer. I'm wondering how Karnstein, Hrubesch and Berger will react when this turns out to a bleeding wild goose chase.'

'Quite honestly, I'm past caring. I feel as sick as a dog. Came on just now. Felt fine until we saw those heads.'

'That was enough to make anyone feel ill,' said Rudi. 'Actually, you do look pretty rough. You've lost a lot of weight. Hell, we all have. But you're definitely a lot skinnier than you were yesterday. You should rest for a while, get some food down you.'

'Not hungry. Come on, let's get moving while I can still stand upright. I really don't like the look of that sky. Another kilometre and we'll take a break then.' Jochen started walking, not really bothered if anyone followed him or not. He hadn't gone a hundred metres before there was a loud thunderclap and a flash of lightning. Then the heavens opened and he was blundering through torrential rain, the likes of which he'd never seen. Within minutes the narrow trail, now winding up a slight incline, became a slick and treacherous ribbon of watery mud. Already tired and weak, weighed down by soaking wet clothing and his heavy bags, rain pouring from his sodden cap and into his eyes, Jochen was unable to keep his footing. Each time he fell to his knees it was an even greater struggle to stand up again. After the fifth time, drenched through and liberally coated in mud, he'd had enough. 'To hell with this,' he told Rudi. 'We need to get off the path and into the trees, wait this out. Otherwise we'll be slipping and sliding all over the damned place. Pass it back down the line. Get in the trees, right-hand side. Tell them to be sure to keep the trail in sight and not go too far in.'

The birch canopy afforded some shelter from the teeming rain, diverting and channelling the water into scattered cascades and a mist of droplets. But it was better to endure the drizzle rather than that relentless downpour. Jochen huddled against the trunk of a particularly large and leafy tree, shivering with cold as he lit a cigarette, thanking his lucky stars that he'd thought to bring an oilskin pouch to keep his Ecksteins and his precious Haushaltsware matches dry. He was running low on both, no more than a week's supply of either remaining. He was going to have a hard time of it if they didn't tie up this mission and get back to civilisation soon.

Under the trees it was dark and gloomy as well as chilly and wet, relieved only by the occasional flicker of lightning. The only sounds were the rumble of thunder, muffled curses as men sought refuge from the rain, and the bizarre braying whinny of the disconsolate mules. *What a miserable place. I'd give anything for birdsong or a woman's voice, a child's laughter.* Thoroughly depressed and feeling utterly exhausted, Jochen slid down the tree until he was squatting on his haunches. He flicked the cigarette butt into a clump of dull, scrawny ferns, folded his arms, closed his eyes and drifted into an uneasy sleep, not stirring when Rudi returned.

The rain stopped an hour and a half later. Rudi shook Jochen awake, stepping smartly aside when his friend immediately threw up. Jochen drank some water and smoked a cigarette, but was unable to rid himself of the aftertaste. He gazed questioningly at Rudi. 'Is it still raining?'

Rudi wiped beads of moisture from his cheeks and forehead. 'No, it's me – I'm sweating like a bastard, and I feel really fucking hot.'

'I'm freezing. Whatever you're going down with probably isn't the same as what I've got. Have you checked the trail?'

'Better than it was. Still muddy and slippery but there's no rain to make it worse underfoot, and the slope isn't too steep. Just as well, because most of the others are sick again. Funny thing is, they all have different symptoms. Headaches, fever, sore throats, coughing and sneezing, abdominal pain, vomiting and aching muscles, in various combinations. Berger's got the shits something terrible, poor old bastard. It could be the flu, I suppose. If it is, fuck knows how we've caught it. We haven't seen anyone else in weeks.'

'Can they walk?'

'I reckon so. Mind you, Berger will probably need to take his strides off completely if he's going to get further than two metres. They've been up and down like a fucking yo-yo.'

Jochen's weary sigh became a wracking cough. 'Alright, tell the men to get ready to move before we all drop dead. Let's find somewhere to put the tents up.'

Before Rudi could move, Karnstein came trampling

through the undergrowth, his expression grim and angry. It took only a minute and a few words for the cause of his distress to become clear. Lorenz and Ziegler were missing.

Filthy, rubber-legged and gasping for breath, they struggled to ascend even that gentle upward slope. The column grew ragged as men lagged behind through weariness, or stopped to vomit or deal with bowels that seemed permanently loose but never emptied. Meanwhile, the new muleteers wrestled with their obstreperous animals, none of which seemed prepared to continue. They managed another half a kilometre before Jochen realised they had no choice but to stop. Even Hrubesch and Berger, who would normally have griped about stopping while it was still light enough to walk on, were vocally grateful for the opportunity to pitch their tent and crawl inside.

Jochen foraged for some relatively dry twigs, leaves and branches, and sacrificed three of his matches to light a fire. He allowed himself the luxury of an extra cigarette on top of his self-imposed daily ration while he took stock of the situation. Fourteen men left. Two officers, two as yet useless members of the Ahnenerbe or Vril Society – *Take your pick*, he thought wryly – and six men looking after the mules. Realistically, that left only four men to protect the sides and rear of the column when they moved, and with two men on each shift it meant longer stints on sentry duty at night. In his mental ledger the debit column grew longer. The only entry on the credit side was the additional food for survivors now that another two men had vanished into thin air. Or been spirited away into some cannibal's larder.

He had just opened a tin of preserved meat and set it

over the fire to heat when Rudi appeared and dropped something in his lap – three full packs of Eckstein cigarettes.

Jochen looked up. 'Where did you get these?'

'Found two in Ziegler's pack and one in Lorenz's.' Rudi shrugged. 'The others shared out their ammo, food and blankets, so I thought as commanding officer you should have their snout. With a daily stipend for the finder, of course.' He became pensive. 'Poor Lorenz. I was only talking to him yesterday. Now I wish I'd been a bit easier on him.'

'Don't torment yourself with hindsight, Rudi. You weren't to know. Anyway, how are you feeling?'

Rudi opened a tin and placed it next to Jochen's meal-in-progress, adding sage and Pfifferlinge to both tins and giving them a cursory stir with his conspicuously clean, shiny spoon. 'Almost human. Bloody hungry, though. You?'

'Yes, I'm much better now that we've stopped. Weird how it came on so suddenly after finding those heads.'

'Same thing happened to everybody,' said Rudi. 'Karnstein said it spread through the column from the front like a wave, front to back. Did you ever see *Nosferatu*? Murnau portrayed Count Orlok as a kind of walking disease. He didn't just drink people's blood, he made them waste away with sickness. A pestilence.'

Jochen stared at him. 'For God's sake, Rudi. Are you telling me you're starting to believe this Baba Yaga nonsense?'

'Of course not. I'm not a complete fucking idiot. No, what I'm trying to say is that maybe all those old vampire stories are really about disease – typhus or cholera or tuberculosis or whatever – stories told by superstitious peasants who embellished symptoms and added an imaginary figure that personified death. Perhaps a relative who died of that disease and reappeared after they died as a pale, gaunt figure like Death in medieval art. Just like Dracula or Orlok in the films.'

'That's an interesting notion.'

'There's more where that came from. Now take that Baba Yaga character. Imagine it's the same sort of thing – death personified – and that it relates to a sickness, a disease that isn't spread from one person to another but is caused by contact with a *place*. A place in the taiga that can make you ill if you so much as walk there and breathe the air. Like that old theory about how disease was spread. What was it called?'

'Miasma. Unhealthy vapours.'

'That's the one. So Baba Yaga represents the miasma that causes sickness in parts of the forest. The idea spreads and grows. It gets enhanced by what people see in fever dreams. Soon Baba Yaga has a whole mythology of her own, like vampires in the Balkans.'

'And you think we stumbled into one of these miasmas.'

'More than once, I'd say. Jochen, we've had no contact with other people for weeks, so we can't have caught anything. And we may be filthy dirty, but the men keep their billycans, knives and spoons clean. I do it and I've seen you do it. Good old SS discipline may turn men into vicious arseholes but it makes basic food hygiene automatic. The upshot is that there's no way we should be getting sick like this. Yet, we wander into a place and we get ill; we leave it and get better. That's empirical evidence, mate. It's *miasma*. The only possible alternative is that one of us is deliberately poisoning the rest – and all of us have been very sick, so I consider that extremely unlikely, especially when everything we eat is tinned or tightly wrapped.'

'I haven't been that ill.'

Rudi laughed. 'You haven't? Take a good look at yourself. You've lost a ridiculous amount of weight. We all have. Most of us are walking skeletons, as weak as kittens. This bastard forest is killing us by inches. It's got to be down to miasma. That or...' He trailed off, pretending to concentrate on stirring his tin of garnished meat.

'Or what?'

'Or Baba Yaga is fucking *real*.'

'But you don't believe that.'

'Of course I fucking don't. So it's got to be miasma, right?'

Jochen attended to his own meal. It was as ready as it was going to be. 'Could be. Or maybe we're being poisoned after all. But not by any of the men.' He took a tentative nibble. The meat was hot enough to eat but not so hot it would burn his mouth. He shovelled in a whole spoonful. The mushrooms and sage made a glorious difference. 'Maybe someone is sneaking into the camp at night and tainting our canteens, putting in something that makes us ill but wears off quickly and doesn't kill us. You can get laxatives and emetics from any pharmacy, and there's plenty of herbs and mushrooms that would do the trick growing wild in most forests.'

Rudi raised an eyebrow. 'Who would do something like that?'

'The cannibals?'

Rudi gazed disgustedly down at his still-cold tin. 'Thank you for that, you cheerful sod. You've put me right off my fucking dinner. Not that it took much effort.' He looked around in mock mystification. 'Where's a bastard wine waiter when you need one?'

Then the uneasy evening quiet was shattered by an excited, jubilant shout.

9

The men were swearing and peering angrily out of their tents to see what was causing the commotion ruining their early night. When they did, they couldn't believe their eyes. Hrubesch was yelling incoherently and dancing like a dervish around the tent he shared with Berger. In his right hand, the pendulum spun rapidly, so fast that centrifugal force kept the silver chain almost parallel with the ground and the iron bob was just a blur. Berger stood to one side, seemingly poised to catch his colleague if Hrubesch tripped and fell toward their campfire.

Jochen noticed that Hrubesch, once rather portly, was now as skinny as any of the others. *Rudi was right. Walking skeletons, all of us.* He pushed the disturbing thought to the back of his mind and took Berger by the arm. 'What the hell is going on?'

'We're almost there,' Berger replied, stony-faced. 'The pendulum indicates that we are in very close proximity to the target.'

'How close?'

'It's not an exact science, but I would say we should arrive at her location in the morning.' Berger frowned. 'At a guess, that would be at the top of this rise. Nearby, at any rate.'

'You don't seem very pleased about it. Not like him.' Jochen pointed to Hrubesch, now on his knees and cackling like a gleeful lunatic.

Berger licked his lips nervously. 'Perhaps I am reconsidering the wisdom of this mission,' he said quietly. 'Perhaps I am beginning to think acquiring Baba Yaga to ensure the Reich's victory may not be worth the risk to the rest of the world.'

'Don't let Hrubesch or Karnstein hear you say that. They'll have you shot as a traitor.'

Berger's laughter was hollow. 'Yes, they most certainly would. And they would be right to do so. Moments of weakness are not permissible. We must not forget our duties, our responsibilities, our purpose. Our *destiny*.' He straightened and stood tall. 'Hauptsturmführer, at daybreak you will order the men to first eat then clean themselves up as best they can and to wear their full uniforms. And every man is to have a haircut. They're looking more like a bunch of Nollendorfplatz nancy boys than the cream of Aryan manhood.' He smiled wanly. 'We need to make the right impression. Proud soldiers, not slovenly vagabonds. All supplies will remain here, except for a day's rations and water, to be carried in their belt pouches. The Lee-Enfields too will be left here – instead the men will be armed with their MP 40s, good German weapons. Once we leave this camp, Hrubesch and I shall be in command and you will obey our instructions immediately and without question. We have written orders from Reichsführer Himmler. They will be destroyed when we acquire our target but you may inspect them now if you require confirmation.'

Jochen grinned. 'That won't be necessary. To be honest, it'll be a relief to have someone else making the decisions. And it'll be an even bigger relief to get this show over with and get back to Germany.'

Berger looked away. 'Do you have a family, Hauptsturmführer Dietrich? A wife and children? A sweetheart?'

'No. There was a girl but… The war, you know. I was away too long, another man swept her off her feet. An older man, a munitions factory manager. I suppose she got sick of wondering if I'd come home in a coffin or minus a limb or two, if I came home at all. No hard feelings, though. In her place I'd have done the same. But Rudi has a girlfriend. Well, three actually, on rotation. He always was a greedy sod. How about you?'

'A wife, a son and two daughters. Wolfgang is in the Ahnenerbe, still single, though I hope not for too long. My daughters are married to SS officers, fine men like you.'

If you only knew. 'You must miss them.'

'More than anything, Hauptsturmführer. I hope I shall see them again.'

'I'm sure you will. We'll do our best to make that happen, to get everyone home.'

Jochen was surprised to realise he meant it. And it wasn't only a matter of getting through the mission in one piece. He wanted every combatant to survive the war and get home to a peaceful life with their loved ones – German,

American, British, French and Italian, even the damned Soviets; the good and the bad, the brave and the timid and the mad. He'd seen too much death and suffering, too much desperation and fear, and he didn't want to see any more. The chances of that, he knew, were slimmer than his depleted waistline.

The new so-called dress uniforms were not the usual formal wear but a variation on typical battledress. They were black, like the old pre-war SS uniforms, not the field-grey of the Waffen-SS. Those worn by Hrubesch and Berger were similar, though cut differently and bereft of insignia except for polished steel swastikas on the collar where runes would normally be. Everyone had a standard SS red armband with a black swastika in a white circle. Jochen's uniform was quite comfortable. Others felt differently.

'Jesus Christ on a motorbike,' said Rudi, pulling a face as he plucked frantically at his crotch. 'These sodding uniform trousers chafe worse than the other buggers. I'll be singing soprano by noon. And as for these poxy jackboots, I'm going to have blisters the size of goose eggs. Mind you, it could be worse. At least we're not wearing tin hats as well. I've never seen Karnstein in a helmet before. He looks like a tortoise. A really fucking ugly tortoise.'

Jochen smiled and stretched. 'I'm just glad we won't have to be carting our packs around today. I feel so light I could float away on the breeze.'

'You look a lot better, too. Got a bit of colour back in your cheeks. And the others have stopped coughing and puking and rushing into the trees for a shit every five minutes.'

'Yes, it feels almost normal. We could be on a training exercise in the Black Forest.'

Rudi snorted. 'This feels normal? Bullshit. Sitting in a bar and flirting with the barmaid is normal, Jochen. Going to work in the morning and coming home in the evening, having a good meal and sleeping in a cosy bed after earning an honest mark is normal. Wandering around fucking Siberia dressed up as toy soldiers and chasing vampires is anything *but* normal. God, these bastard trousers are driving me round the bend. Thank Christ that idiot Hrubesch hasn't got us goose-stepping. That would just about finish off the Brandt family jewels.'

'You know, it reminds me of that holiday we had in England. What was the name of that forest we trekked through the year before Hitler took over? Up near Newcastle-upon-Tyne?'

'Kielder. More of a copse compared to this place. Just as creepy, though this terrain is much rougher, all rocks and troughs. Actually, this puts me more in mind of that place in the Ukraine.'

Jochen blanched. 'Christ, I wish you hadn't said that. Brings me out in a cold sweat just thinking about it. All those bodies…'

'…and they wanted us to add to the pile. Mopping up, they said. Sheer fucking insanity. I mean, couldn't they see what had happened? What they were about to do?'

'We did the right thing, Rudi.'

Rudi sighed. 'Yeah, and this is our reward. Sometimes I wish we'd just thrown our weapons down and let that evil motherfucker Schumacher shoot us.'

'Speak for yourself. This is better than being dead,

Rudi.'

Rudi pulled a face, bent his legs and adjusted his crotch once more. 'You reckon?'

They made their way to where the Sturmmänner were lined up, ready for Hrubesch's inspirational speech. Jochen was pleasantly surprised when the Ahnenerbe man kept it short and more or less to the point.

'My fellow Germans, today we reach the culmination of our mission. In many ways, it is a short journey into the unknown, toward a mystery that will bring us victory and usher in a glorious new era for the Reich and for mankind. What you are about to witness will be outside your experience, perhaps even disturbing, even to battle-hardened men such as you. But I know that you, as soldiers of the Reich and exemplars of the Aryan race, will remain calm and stand firm no matter what may transpire, and obey all orders exactly and with alacrity. That is all. Now, let us march.' Hrubesch gestured to Jochen and Rudi, indicating that they should take their place at the head of the depleted column.

'Fucking nutter,' Rudi muttered.

'Today the nutter outranks us,' Jochen reminded him. 'We play along, right? Come on, let's get this stupidity over with and then we can go home.'

The march – more a ragged procession of men barely strong enough to stand, and mules displaying their trademark stubbornness – didn't take long. The path ascended toward an uneven plateau, and went on in a dead straight line for another hundred metres or so. After only fifteen minutes they stood on the lip of a roughly circular valley about a kilometre across and perhaps forty metres deep, the sides sloping gently to a more or less flat plain devoid of trees. The only signs of life were a few patches of low scrub and sparse clumps of coarse grasses, and an indistinct but obviously artificial structure standing in the centre.

'What is that?' Jochen asked. His head was buzzing unpleasantly.

'Buggered if I know,' Rudi replied. 'We should have brought some field glasses. Shit, my head feels weird, all itchy on the inside, like it's full of beetles or ants or something. And my guts are churning again.'

'Same here. Maybe it's the altitude?'

Rudi laughed shakily. 'This is Siberia, not the fucking Himalayas. We can't be more than a hundred metres above sea level.'

Hrubesch and Berger joined them at the valley's rim. Hrubesch pointed at the central structure. 'There – that is where we must go. The folktales tell of Baba Yaga's hut. That must be it.'

But when they got there, they found it wasn't a hut at all. The structure was a layered pyramid of human bones, long bones from arms and legs stacked neatly and carefully, the spaces between them packed with scapulae, ribs and smaller bones from hands and feet. The bottom layer was about three metres square, the top a metre to a side. At each corner, a metre from the pyramid, wooden poles had been erected, crudely decorated with pelvic bones and vertebrae. Seven human skulls were arranged at the pyramid's summit, surrounding a bone carved into the shape of a large phallus, with six more skulls around the pyramid's base. The bones were mostly brown with age, speckled with moss and lichen. The skulls at the top seemed discoloured and malformed. The skulls around the base, though, still bore much of their original flesh. And they had clearly been thoroughly gnawed.

'Fuck,' said Rudi. 'Those are our missing men, including the latest absconders. I thought we left most of those back on the trail?'

'We did,' said Jochen. 'We all saw Karnstein cover up the first four. Whoever took them in the first place must have gone back for them after we'd moved on.'

'Fucking cannibals. This is a bad place, Jochen. Let's get the fuck out of here.'

'We don't need to worry about cannibals, Rudi. Twelve men with MP 40s, and even Hrubesch and Berger have pistols. If the cannibals attack, we'll be ready for them. We'll blow them away before they have a chance to warm up the oven.'

Hrubesch and Berger were examining the bones, the former taking photographs from various angles with what appeared to be a brand-new Leica, the latter bending over, sketchbook in hand, and peering closely at the pyramid. 'The skulls have been painted,' said Berger. 'Natural pigments, red ochre and charcoal mixed with egg white, at a guess. Black for the cranium, red for the cheeks and jaw. From the thickness, I'd say they've been periodically renewed. Not for a while, though. And look – animal horns have been glued onto them with what appears to be pine resin. Musk deer, I think. The phallus is, I believe, carved from a human femur and is coated with what looks like dried blood. Fascinating. Primitive religious symbolism. I'd say this is an altar.' He scratched at his scalp. 'Is anyone else having trouble with these damned insects?'

There were no insects in sight. Yet every man there had his cap or shiny new helmet askew, fingers frantically rubbing or scratching at his head. Most were also waving their free hands to ward off invisible flies or wasps. Seeing this, Hrubesch replaced his own cap and brusquely called the men to attention. 'You are soldiers of the Reich,' he barked. 'Comport yourselves with dignity. This is merely an infestation of mites, too small to be seen with the naked eye. An irritation, nothing more.'

Jochen and Rudi exchanged glances. Mites? That insistent itching and scraping was *inside* their heads, not on their skin or in their hair. And mites did not buzz angrily like wasps or hum like bumblebees. The men seemed equally sceptical as they strove to remain still and stand erect. But incredulity was the least of it. They all looked deeply afraid.

10

The swastika flag was in place and almost fluttering in a feeble breeze. Though pleased to be rid of that part of his burden, Jochen wasn't happy with much else. 'Why have you got the men lined up like that? If we're attacked they'll be sitting ducks. We should be securing the valley, setting up a perimeter. Well, as best we can with so few of us.'

'Reichsführer Himmler's instructions were very clear,' said Hrubesch. 'We are to treat this as a formal meeting between the Reich and a potential ally. That means correct military presentation, and no actions or gestures that might be considered hostile.'

Jochen rolled his eyes. 'With respect, Himmler isn't here. He doesn't have to consider that the Red Army might appear at any moment and put a bullet up his back passage. He hasn't had men snatched by headhunters and cannibals.'

'Nevertheless, those are our orders. We present ourselves appropriately and await contact.'

'It's the middle of the afternoon,' Rudi pointed out.

'Don't vampires only come out at night? How long do the men have to stand there like that? Until tomorrow morning?'

'If necessary,' Hrubesch replied.

Rudi turned to Jochen. 'This is bollocks,' he growled. 'This idiot is full of shit. Flags and fucking parades, my arse. The men have to eat and rest, and be ready to fight. The fucking Ivans and the bastard cannibals won't wait for us to finish our little parade before they start shooting or consulting their recipe books.' He brandished his MP 40 and glared at Hrubesch. 'You can go screw yourself, you old fool. Obersturmführer Rudolf Brandt is *not* on the fucking menu.'

Hrubesch drew his pistol, a Walther P38, and thrust it toward Rudi's face. 'You will obey the Reichsführer's orders,' he snarled. 'You will obey *my* orders.'

Shocked, Jochen stepped between them. 'Obersturmführer, Hrubesch – stop this at once. Please lower your weapons.'

Rudi and Hrubesch continued to lock eyes, their mouths twisted into grimaces of rage and hatred. For a moment, Jochen feared they would start shooting, not caring that he was between them. Then Rudi lowered his MP 40 and ran a shaky left hand across his eyes. 'Forgive me,' he said quietly. 'It's this itching in my head. It's driving me out of my fucking mind. Makes me want to scream.'

Hrubesch's gun hand fell limply to his side. Chest heaving, he gazed down at the barren soil. 'I too must apologise. This place is… most unsettling. I believe it is her presence, an emanation of some sort. Negative Vril, perhaps. But you are right, Obersturmführer. Tell the men to take half an hour to rest, and to eat. As the Hauptsturmführer said, we do not have enough men to properly set up a secure perimeter, but we can post four look-outs at the valley rim, one at each of the cardinal points. That is the best we can do in the circumstances.'

The Sturmmänner were still at attention, though twitching hands, clenched fists and shifty, darting eyes betrayed their tension. Some were casting murderous glances at those nearest them. Jochen removed his cap and scratched his head. 'The men are at boiling point. Look at them – they're all scared witless and spoiling for a fight at the same time. They need something to keep them occupied, take their minds off this abominable...' He closed his eyes and scratched harder. 'Whatever the hell it is.'

'I agree,' said Hrubesch. 'But, short of sending all of them to the valley rim to keep watch, I do not know what to suggest.'

'Get them to take a closer look at the lower valley wall,' Rudi suggested. 'There may be fissures, caves. If this is Baba Yaga's place, she has to live somewhere, right?'

'The folktales say she has a hut.' said Hrubesch stubbornly.

Rudi snorted derisively. 'Yeah, Berger told me. Apparently it moves around on chicken legs. I expect she usually keeps it parked next to that nice house made of gingerbread.'

'Speaking of Berger,' said Jochen thoughtfully. 'He doesn't seem as affected by this... this *thing* as the rest of us.'

'That's because he's focused on the bone altar,' said

Hrubesch. 'He's a very single-minded man. When Heinz becomes interested in something the rest of world might as well not exist.'

'You know him well?'

'Since childhood. Heinz is only a few years my senior, and we were neighbours in Berlin. Our fathers were founding members of the Vril Society.'

'How far back does the Society go?'

'It was founded in 1890, when a group of eminent scholars – all known to one another – each independently experienced apocalyptic visions of the Aryan race mongrelised and corrupted beyond redemption by subhumans. In the beginning it was known as the Volksursprüngegesellschaft, and the purpose was to investigate the history and nature of precognition and related psychic phenomena, but the name has changed as our aims and interests developed. We became the Vril Society in 1929. We have used other names in our interaction with the wider world. For instance, in the 1920s we sometimes called ourselves the Wahrheitsgesellschaft, and in 1925 we began publishing selected materials under the name Reichsarbeitsgemeinschaft. And, of course, in 1918 we created the Thule Society, and through that the Ahnenerbe.'

'That's a lot of influence for a group no-one's ever heard of,' said Jochen.

'Actually, we are quite well known. Rumour is a kind of fame, is it not? And you will undoubtedly recognise a few individual names. Karl Haushofer, Ernst Schertel, Josef Mengele and former Reichsleiter Hess, for example. The rest of us prefer to stay out of the limelight.'

"Rudolf Hess is a member?' Jochen was astonished. 'But he's a traitor.'

'Hess lost his nerve – and perhaps his mind – when the Society attempted to enlist the help of non-human agencies in the war effort. What you might call angelic or demonic entities. We failed, and nearly all of us came to the conclusion that such beings have no objective existence. But Hess began to experience delusions, hallucinations that led him to treason. Unfortunately, he is still a member. Our rules are inviolable. Only death can end membership, and there are always to be exactly nine of us, to reflect both the nine worlds of ancient Germanic cosmology and the Ennead, the nine pre-eminent gods of ancient Egypt. Fortunately, we are also only a rumour to the Führer, or our association with Hess might have had disastrous consequences. Himmler knows of us, though he deals with us only through the Ahnenerbe and Thule Society. Normally he would follow our instructions. However, we must cede to his rank in operational matters. It is inconvenient, but the Reichsführer is almost always amenable to our suggestions.'

Rudi laughed. 'I must say, you're being pretty talkative for a member of a very secretive secret society.'

Hrubesch shrugged. 'Soon secrecy will be immaterial. When we acquire the services of the woman we know as Baba Yaga, the Reich's victory will be assured. Then, we shall reveal ourselves to the world. And if we fail – well, then it will not matter one way or another. The Reich will fall, to the Soviets, the British and Americans, the French. The Allies will not forgive what we have done in the name of Aryan purity and the supremacy of the Reich.'

Jochen had a sudden thought. 'What's in it for her?'

'I beg your pardon?' Hrubesch peered up at him distractedly.

'Well, we know what the Reich gets out of any deal you make with her. A weapon and potential breeding material for more of the same. But what does Baba Yaga get in return?'

Hrubesch smiled, a strange rictus halfway between smugness and terror. 'That remains to be seen, Hauptsturmführer. That remains to be seen.' He walked off to join Berger, who was wholly engrossed in examining and sketching the altar of bones.

The men found nothing of interest in their exploration of the valley's sides. No caves, cracks or artificial holes, no animal burrows. Only densely compacted rock and soil. The circular formation was a half-hearted bone of contention. Hrubesch favoured a volcanic origin for the valley; Berger asserted it was a crater left by an ancient meteorite. Jochen and Rudi listened to their bickering from a distance.

'It could be a latrine dug by a fucking giant for all I care,' said Rudi dismissively. 'Honestly, Hrubesch is a moron. A child could see that this valley isn't volcanic. No sign of lava flows, pumice, obsidian or anything else normally associated with volcanism. Unless someone actually took the time and effort to dig this out, my money's on the meteorite.'

'You really did pay attention in geography classes, didn't you?'

'It was that or get my arse whipped raw by that pervert Vennemann. One taste of his cane was enough for me, mate. Actually, it wasn't so much the pain as the look of pleasure on his face after he'd given me a bloody good thrashing. I never gave the old bastard a second opportunity. Hrubesch reminds me of Vennemann. Same buttoned-up, sour-faced, slightly seedy look. Mind you, all the top Nazis have that, except Göring. Makes me wonder what the Reich would be like if he'd become Führer instead of Adolf. Mandatory cigar-smoking, gourmet meals and drunkenness, probably. I could live with that. Mind you, it wouldn't have done the Jews any good. Fat Hermann's as bad as the others on that count. He's made a fucking lot of money out of the Jews, the arsehole.'

'Keep your voice down.'

'Fuck it, I don't care anymore,' said Rudi despondently. 'Any of these fuckers so much as look at me the wrong way, I'll put a fucking bullet in them. Fuck the lot of them. Between them, the chafing and this constant bastard itching inside my skull, I've just about had enough.'

Jochen's mind was filled with images from long ago. Late afternoon, a ravine in a forest not unlike the Siberian taiga. The ragged line of Jews, women and children the earlier Einsatzgruppen had missed. Jews he and Rudi had helped round up. The women weeping and resigned, the kids' eyes wide with fear. The sadistic Hauptsturmführer Schumacher, lips wet with an unholy excitement, blood already on his hands and face from beatings he had personally administered, ordering the robotic Sturmmänner to take aim. That single appalled look he'd exchanged with Rudi, the sudden knowledge that this was something they could not allow to happen, the line they could not cross. His finger on the trigger of his MP 40. And thirty seconds later, nineteen erstwhile comrades dead and sixty or seventy Jews who would live at least one day longer, melting into the forest like ghosts. 'How did we get away with it?' he wondered aloud.

Lies, that was how. The non-existent partisans who'd surprised them at the ravine, the fictitious fight for survival, the imaginary revenge exacted upon the despicable Jews and treacherous Ivans. The very real long journey back to their own lines, careful to avoid both Soviet and German forces. Finally deciding it would be better to face a court martial and risk a firing squad than suffer what the Ivans would do to them if they were caught. Then discovering that their lies were aided and abetted by a needy sort of gullibility. Superior officers and the likes of Himmler and Hitler wanted to believe their story, eager to incorporate their heroic exploits into the greater Nazi narrative. Medals and promotion followed. And so their brief, impulsive moral victory brought its own punishment – that constant, nagging sense of shame, the secret stigma of basking in a glory that was utterly fraudulent. Guilt, too, at taking lives even to save the innocent. And inevitably, always, the fear of discovery. Just thinking about it made him sick to his stomach.

And now this madness. Although, thinking about it, hadn't his war been one long bout of delirium anyway? He'd read somewhere that one sign of insanity was seeing patterns where there were none. Since the rise of Hitler, his country had descended into chaos masquerading as order, guided by delusion dressed up as reason. The only way to survive was by pretending to embrace it, and it was only a short step from pretence to acceptance. Perhaps it was inevitable that one day derangement would engulf him as it had swallowed so many others, that the toxic fantasy would become his reality too. So wasn't it appropriate that the nameless demons which had haunted him since Babi Yar should be made manifest in this place with no name – that Babi Yar should inexorably lead him to Baba Yaga? The names even sounded horribly alike. That couldn't be mere coincidence, surely. It must mean *something*. An omen? A pointer toward his destiny? That was said to be another sign of insanity – believing that God or fate had singled you out for a special purpose. Jochen smiled bleakly and reached for a cigarette.

Then, the impossible happened. The air between him and the altar seemed to tremble and shimmer, rippling the late afternoon shadows cast by the poles and that grisly stack of bones ten metres away. Unable to comprehend what he was seeing, Jochen froze, staring mindlessly as one shadow somehow turned itself inside-out and revealed a figure that simply hadn't been there a split-second before.

11

She was tall for a woman – Jochen estimated her height at about one and three-quarter metres – and slender though voluptuous, with very pale skin, long, loose golden hair, red lips and eyes so blue and clear that they seemed to glow with an inner light. She was, he thought, probably the loveliest woman he had ever seen. But for all her beauty, she did not attract him sexually. She wore a ragged, filthy dress that had once been white, a dress that might have been fashionable decades ago; and she stank horribly, a repellent mixture of chlorine, ordure, bad eggs and rotting flesh, the reek assailing his nostrils as though the distance between them had somehow shrunk to nothing.

'How the fuck – ?' The voice seemed to come from a long way away. Jochen couldn't tell who had spoken.

The woman, who looked no older than her late teens or early twenties, gazed at them frankly, studying each man in turn. Her eyes oscillated rapidly, yet almost imperceptibly, in their sockets; her nostrils flared and quivered like those of a scenting hound. Then she smiled, her teeth white as fresh snow, and the examination ceased. 'So many of you,' she said in fluent but strangely-accented German. 'I suppose I should be flattered that so many have travelled so far to see me.'

Hesitantly, Hrubesch took a step toward her. 'You are the one they call Baba Yaga?'

She laughed musically. 'I have heard the stories. On my travels I hear many things. But you are mistaken. Those stories of Baba Yaga are centuries older than me. The peasant imagination projects what little it knows onto that which it does not understand. My name is Irina. You are Hrubesch.' She laughed again, pointed a finger at them, one by one. 'Hrubesch, Berger, Dietrich, Brandt, Karnstein... I know all your names, and more.'

Hrubesch flinched. 'How?'

She seemed disappointed. 'For such a learned man you are rather obtuse, Herr Hrubesch. You are here for a purpose, are you not? A proposition for me, yes?'

Hrubesch nodded dumbly, clearly beguiled by the woman. And, Jochen knew, wholly out of his depth. For a long minute, they all stood there in silence, the men staring at the woman, she meeting their gaze, one at a time, her eyes lingering longest on Jochen and Rudi. Finally, Berger cleared his throat and spoke. 'Miss – Irina – perhaps you would care to join Hrubesch and myself for a private conversation?'

This jolted Hrubesch from his trance. 'Yes, indeed,' he muttered. 'Hauptsturmführer Dietrich, please tell the men to leave the valley at once. You and the Obersturmführer may join them.' The last was not a suggestion.

Jochen conveyed Hrubesch's order and took up the rear as they ascended the slope. Rudi caught his eye and grinned wanly. It was only when he saw how badly his friend was shaking that he realised he was trembling too.

'How did she do that?' Rudi asked. 'It was as if she just popped out of the shadows. Gave me a right fucking shock. I nearly shit myself.'

'I don't know,' admitted Jochen. 'Never seen anything like it before. But it has to be a trick, an illusion. You remember that magician we saw in Berlin? The Amazing Rotwang? To this day I can't work out how he made that bird cage vanish, and when he started eating those razor blades I was sure he was going to slice his tongue to ribbons. And when he turned that metal statue into a living woman…Well, that was astonishing. I couldn't see where he made the switch.'

'Yeah, but stage magicians use, what do they call it, misdirection. You're focusing on one thing while they doing something else. We weren't focusing on anything, Jochen.'

'Oh, but we were. The itching in our heads, arguing with Hrubesch and worrying about being caught in the open by the Ivans. And that horrible altar thing is a distraction all by itself. Stalin could have marched through with a brass band and we might not have noticed.'

Rudi wasn't convinced. 'There's still something not quite right about that Irina. She's a good-looking woman but I really don't think I could stand her company for long. She stinks to high heaven, for one thing. And she makes my flesh crawl. I reckon she's well and truly off her rocker. Is she the cannibal, do you think?'

'There's no one else out here,' said Jochen. 'Unless she has other people hidden away and lying in wait for us, ready to pounce if we let our guard down. What do cannibals look like anyway? Like you and me, probably, until they get the knives and forks out.'

Rudi shrugged a qualified agreement. 'I'll tell you one thing, though. She's not a vampire, or a werewolf, or even Baba fucking Yaga. I don't believe in any of that bollocks, Jochen. Shit, I don't even believe in God. But how did she know our names? And how come she speaks German?'

'Obviously she knows our names because she's been following us for a while and listening to our conversations. You heard her. She was taking the piss out of Hrubesch because he didn't even *consider* that might be how she knew. He wants her to possess supernatural abilities. Anyway, why shouldn't she speak German? Lots of people know more than one language. Mind you, her German is a bit odd. The way she talks reminds me of my great-grandfather on my mum's side, who died when I was nine. Old-fashioned and with a slight accent, as if he was a foreigner, though he was born and raised in Leipzig and never travelled further than Dresden. I suppose language changes over time, like fashion and art. Maybe she was taught German by someone very old who didn't bother keeping up.'

They smoked in silence for a while. Jochen was down to his last pack of Eckstein, but took some comfort in his assumption that the mission was near completion and he would soon be back in Germany, where SS officers had only minor difficulty obtaining supplies of cigarettes. Eventually, Jochen walked a short distance and pissed against a tree. When he rejoined Rudi, Hrubesch and Berger were hauling themselves out of the valley and onto the plateau.

'She wants to speak with you two,' said Hrubesch between gasps. Despite the deepening twilight Jochen could see the man was as white as a sheet and plainly terrified. Berger looked shocked, and appeared to have lost the power of speech. Peering over Hrubesch's shoulder, he caught Jochen's eye and silently shook his head when he saw Jochen open his mouth to speak. *Don't*, he mouthed, his eyes wide and frantic.

Jochen sniffed. One of them, perhaps both, had soiled himself. And each had vomit on his uniform jacket. Puzzled, Jochen frowned and cocked his head, inviting an explanation, but Berger had turned away and covered his face with both hands. 'How did it go?'

''She has agreed to accompany us back to the Reich, Hauptsturmführer,' Hrubesch replied without enthusiasm. Jochen was astonished at his lack of celebration. Having found his Baba Yaga, Hrubesch should have been elated. On the contrary, he had the air of a man who had gambled his life savings and lost. 'We have agreed to her terms, as Reichsführer Himmler instructed.'

'What were her terms?'

He was answered by a drawn-out, bloodcurdling scream from the other side of the valley, a wail that was equal parts terror, despair and pain. Berger finally found his voice. 'That was the first instalment,' he whispered, then began to weep.

The woman who called herself Irina was squatting by a small fire a few metres from the bone altar, licking her fingers. Her ragged dress was hitched up, carelessly exposing her upper thighs. Jochen had no desire to see what lay there, or to imagine what she was licking from her hands. Nor did he want to gaze upon that lovely but false face. Aside from Rudi, who now sat cross-legged beside him, facing Irina across the blaze, the only other thing he could see was the altar where, he knew, a seventh severed and gnawed head had been placed in the lower circle. He chose what he thought would be the lesser evil. But when his eyes met Irina's he regretted it immediately and instead turned his gaze to the flames.

'You wished to speak with us?' he asked.

She grinned widely, her teeth and lips and tongue stained red. 'You two are interesting,' she said. 'The others believe unquestioningly in this Führer the man Hrubesch kept talking about, this Reich of yours. But not you, Jochen Dietrich and Rudi Brandt. You don't believe in them at all, do you? And there's another difference. The others reek of cruelty and violence. They remind me of myself, just a little. Yet on you, their leaders, I smell only betrayal and its by-products.' Slowly and deliberately, she stood, holding the hem of dress so that her shapely legs remained fully exposed.

Suddenly, Jochen became very sexually aroused. The groan beside him indicated that the same had happened to Rudi. Irina laughed. 'I can do that whenever I wish,' she told them. 'I have my appetites, gentlemen, my needs; and I have learned how to tempt the most reluctant of men. I can do other things. You'd be amazed at what I can do.'

As abruptly as it had come, Jochen's lust dissipated, leaving him feeling hollow and empty. He licked his cracked lips, refused to ask the obvious question. *How?* 'How did you come to be here? Are there others?'

'I was quite alone until you came. Well, mostly. I came here from Krasnoyarsk with my father. Before that I lived in Petersburg. I wasn't what you'd call a well-behaved girl. I had wide-ranging interests, needs that were thought shocking. My father disapproved and tried to tame me. He's on the altar now.'

'Where do you live?'

Irina laughed again. 'Certainly not in a hut that moves on chicken legs. I have a little cabin just north of here. It has all I require – a bed, a door, shelves. I like to read. Once in a while I go to Krasnoyarsk or Petersburg for books or new dresses. It's getting harder to do that, though. The buildings and streets change so fast. I have to find new shadows.'

'What do you do out here?'

'I read. I roam. I hunt. I *eat*.' She sniffed deeply and smacked her red lips. 'There's really not much else to do. Sometimes I find a man and take my pleasure. If not, there's always my little friend atop the altar. I made him myself, from my father's thigh. Poor Daddy, once was too much for the pious old prude when he was alive – but now he is always ready and willing. Though I try to reserve him for the full moon, when I anoint him with blood, hemlock, nightshade and the juice of those remarkable mushrooms. Then I fly for my master, my creator; and he speaks to me, imbues me with even greater power.'

Jochen's skin crawled with revulsion. 'Your master?'

Irina sensed his horror, smiled demurely. 'More of a mentor, really. He changed me when I came here, so long ago. He made me what I am, which is no more than the potential of my younger flesh, the expression of my heart and mind manifested at last in this meat and bone.' She pointed. 'You see that altar? That is where he fell to earth thousands of years ago, after he was cast out of heaven by the White One, Atem, his ancient twin. He plunged from space and through our air, with horns of smoke and fire, roaring in pain and fury. Beasts ran away and men trembled and cowered in fear. Everyone became sick. The land was made barren and desolate when Sammael fell and was imprisoned deep, deep below the ground. That very spot.'

'Sammael?'

She shrugged. 'He has other names. Lucifer, Satan, Ahriman, Set, Loki... But those are names men speak when they need a god to blame for their cruelty, greed and deceit. Those vices already existed long before he came. He told me that for many years he has been in other places, too. In Arabia and Troy his houses were destroyed by fire and brute force. Ancient sorcerers bound him tightly in his houses in England and the New World. Here too, he was chained like a beast in a zoo, though I unloosed him and he rewarded me.'

'You freed him? What do you mean?'

'As I said, the land was poisoned by his fall. Do you know the Bible? "A great star fell from heaven, blazing like a torch, and it fell on a third of the rivers and on the springs of water. The name of the star is Wormwood. A third of the waters became wormwood, and many died from the water, because it was made bitter." That is just how it was here. People erected silly stones and planted magic herbs to warn others away – and to keep the poison in. One day a shaman came to reclaim his ancestral land, in iron armour and a copper cage for a helmet. The shaman cast spells and hammered an iron spike into the ground, right where the altar is now, and Sammael's power was neutralised: frozen and imprisoned until I found the spike. I was curious and dug it out to see what it was, and so unbound him. That was when Sammael first spoke to me, when he saw my heart and changed my body.'

'Did the transformation hurt?'

She looked at him strangely. 'It was very painful but it was over in minutes. I remember screaming. But I didn't die, if that's what you mean.'

'What does Sammael tell you?'

'He speaks to me of the past and the future, and tells me of things taking place in the present, in far-off places. That is how I know I was not the first person he altered, and that others like me are alive today. One was a mistake.'

Rudi snorted. 'It's just a collection of legends and fairytales. You seem like an educated woman. Surely you don't believe that nonsense.'

Improbably, Irina folded her arms and stamped her right foot. 'Oh, fine,' she said in a bored voice. 'Have it your way. Sammael is one name for an entity that is actually a set of sub-atomic material originating in a universe which exists in a dimension parallel to our own. That universe intersects with ours in the form of infinitesimally small particles or waves, which sometimes become trapped here, locked by accident or design into particular arrangements of magnetic fields and electrical networks, where they may attain localised sentience while remaining linked to its parent universe as well as its other manifestations in our world. When that happens it can then be harnessed to manipulate biological material at the molecular level, so altering the properties of that particular organism. The nature of those changes depends on the personality and intentions of whoever summons or otherwise comes into intimate contact with Sammael. He knows the past, present and future because all his manifestations are in constant communication and, like other such particles, that communication seems to occur both backward and forward in time. However, time is not the straight line or arrow that we perceive it to be. Humans have evolved to imagine time that way for convenience. There. Is that better?'

Rudi's jaw dropped. 'Fucking hell, I think I prefer the story about the hut with chicken legs. At least I could understand that.'

'I told you, I read a lot,' she said. 'Darwin, Einstein, Heisenberg, McTaggart, Hegel, Newton, Bohr, Dirac, Kant, Heisenberg, Swedenborg...' She closed her eyes and licked her lips, shivering slightly as if the names alone were a source of ecstasy. 'I am very intelligent and crave knowledge as an addict longs for morphine or cocaine. And I enjoy poetry, especially Byron and Shelley, Keats and Goethe, men who light in darkness and knew the dark heart of light. I speak and read Russian, English, German and French. The bookshops of Petersburg – I refuse to use the Bolshevik name – are not what they were before the revolution, but still they stock interesting and informative works. I have stolen many, many books and journals over the past two hundred years.'

Jochen raised an eyebrow. 'You claim to have lived for two centuries?'

'It's the eighteenth of September, isn't it? So that would be two hundred and twenty-one years, one month and fifteen days, to be precise.' She sighed theatrically. 'You do not believe me. But then, men do not equate age with beauty, do they? Not for women, at any rate. It is either decrepitude or grandeur, and neither quicken the male pulse like the gorgeous brevity of a woman's youth. "What is this world's delight? Lightning that mocks the night, brief even as bright," as Shelley put it.'

'Well, all that sounds pretty far-fetched,' said Jochen. 'Try to see it from our point of view.'

Slowly, she shook her head, her golden hair undulating hypnotically, red sparks dancing in her blue eyes. 'No, I think you should try to see it from mine.' Her smile broadened and became a grin, and the grin grew into an impossible yawn.

12

Hrubesch and Berger were squatting a long way from the other men, engaged in quiet but intense conversation, when Jochen and Rudi returned, wild-eyed, dishevelled and white-faced. Rudi seized Hrubesch by the throat with one hand, pressed the muzzle of his Luger into the startled man's temple with the other. 'You dirty bastard motherfucker,' he snarled. 'What did you promise her? What does that fucking horrible creature get in return for her services to the bastard Reich, eh? Come on, you shitbag. Out with it, or I'll put a bullet in your fucking head.'

Jochen laid a trembling hand on Rudi's arm. 'Easy, Rudi. He's still in charge, don't forget.'

'In charge, my arse. We know who's in fucking charge now, and it's none of us. Talk, Hrubesch.'

'A camp,' Hrubesch blurted. 'We said she could have a camp while we study her. And…' He fell silent.

Rudi jabbed the Luger's barrel hard into Hrubesch's head. 'And what?'

Berger interrupted. 'And one of the men every night while we travel to Karnstein's rendezvous site. It was that or all of us, here and now. We had no choice but to agree.'

Rudi lowered his weapon and Jochen pulled him aside. 'He's right, Rudi. It's the only way any of us are going to get out of this alive. We've seen what she is.'

'But we can't do that.' Rudi was weeping. 'She's like one of those insects that eats its mate while they're doing it. A praying mantis. A walking fucking nightmare.'

'We heard your screams.' Berger's smile was sickly. 'She showed us only a little of what she can do – what she can *be*. A brief and mild taste, I think, compared with what she seems to have revealed to you.'

Jochen shuddered. 'Oh, she certainly revealed. And you want to take that diseased creature back to Germany?'

'It is for the good of the Reich,' said Hrubesch, rubbing gently at his bruised neck. 'Irina says she is unable to conceive but that does not matter. Mengele has developed a technique for taking genetic material from one person and inserting it into another as an active principle, so that particular traits can be transferred between people.'

'I've heard about fucking Mengele,' said Rudi. 'The grapevine is full of rumours, and I've heard some stuff from very reliable sources. His experiments with twins, cutting up defenceless Jews. The sadistic bastard is just a fucking witch-doctor. Frankenstein without the moral scruples.'

'Mengele has demonstrated his techniques,' Hrubesch insisted. 'In only a few years he and his colleague Sieben Pretorius have transformed our understanding of genetics and developed practical applications. They have taken material from Aryan cells and transferred it to Jewish ova, which become embryos without the need for conventional fertilisation – embryos which are genetically Aryan. They have transplanted what Mengele calls Ursprungzellen, the basal cells from which organs and other tissues develop, from perfect Aryan specimens into men and women of inferior races and transformed them in only a few months – made them bigger and stronger, changed brown hair into fair, turned brown eyes into blue. Imagine what he could achieve with Irina as a source of such genetic material – imagine a whole army with her abilities.'

'Oh, jolly fucking good,' Rudi sneered. 'Break out the bastard bubbly and we can drink a toast to a new world of gods and monsters.'

'An army of cannibalistic maniacs?' Jochen was appalled. 'Murderous creatures who see ordinary people only as so many meals? Who would control them, Hrubesch? Who *could* control them?'

'A few seconds,' Rudi went on, tears still streaming down his face. 'That's all it took to turn us into a pair of nervous wrecks. A few fucking seconds.'

Berger eyed him curiously. 'What did she do to you down there? All she did for us was demonstrate her strength and speed, and that unsettling ability to hop from one shadow to another. It made us – well, very afraid and rather ill. That scratching and buzzing, you know. But that was all. Did she lay hands on you?'

Rudi sank to the ground and sobbed despairingly. Jochen sighed weakly and closed his eyes. 'She didn't so much as touch us. She didn't need to.'

Her smile became a grin, and the grin grew into an impossible yawn.

The irritation in Jochen's cranium intensified, now accompanied by mental images of ants, wasps, beetles and cockroaches, thousand upon thousand, seething inside his head, carapaces and claws scraping at bone and brain tissue. Bile rose in his throat as she opened her mouth like a python preparing to swallow a pig, a gaping cavern crammed with uneven rows of razors and daggers. Her legs and arms, fingers and face elongated, her skin becoming corpse-white and phosphorescent, casting its own light. Her eyes became lamps, so blue and bright that their glow was almost black. In the blink of an eye, she had sprinted a hundred metres into the distance, and was back at the fireside in the same span of time, now standing well over two metres tall, a spindly fever dream of fangs and talons, tongue engorged and lolling, hair writhing like a halo of angry golden serpents, and blackly burning eyes filled with violence and an insane, insatiable lust.

Jochen heard Rudi scream, and realised that he had joined in. As one, the two friends jumped up and ran as fast as they could, but barely made fifty metres before they were forced to stop, dropping their trousers and voiding their bowels. Another fifty metres and they were doubled over, vomiting projectiles of half-digested food and gastric juices, then crawling on hands and knees until they were able to stand upright again. Somewhere along that last stretch, Jochen pissed himself. At the foot of the slope leading out of the valley, they stopped again and at last looked back. They could see the fire and the white figure standing beside it, and heard that musical laughter as she mocked them.

'Nosferatu.' Rudi's awed whisper was cracked and hoarse, and he looked and sounded like a frightened child.

Jochen couldn't disagree. But, although Murnau's eerie film had somehow captured the essence of what Irina had become, it didn't tell the whole story. Others of her kind, he was now certain, those that had been created millennia ago, had inspired myths and legends across the *world. Gorgons, vampires and werewolves were the least of it. Men and women like Irina had once been feared and placated, even venerated by people who, although ordinary, shared her desires – the same unconquerable need to rape, torture and kill, to consume human flesh and blood, to bring terror and misery and despair. Jochen had known men like that. He had served alongside them, taken orders from them. They were the men who now ruled Germany and had rained death and destruction across half the planet. The Third Reich would not only welcome Irina as a saviour – it would worship her as a goddess and the disease she carried would become a pestilential sacrament.*

He took off his uniform jacket and threw it away, vowing never to wear it or anything like it again, now wholly sure of what it would one day represent and finally rejecting all complicity. Rudi, still shaking like a leaf, understood the gesture and did likewise.

'Nosferatu,' Rudi repeated, as they began their ascent and Irina's howling laughter continued to resound across the valley floor.

'We didn't see anything like that,' frowned Berger. 'Are you sure?'

'As sure as I came within one trouser button of shitting my pants,' said Rudi. 'As sure as I pissed myself and threw my fucking guts up. I've never been so scared in my entire life, not even that time at Stalingrad when Zhukov was kicking our arses. And do you want to know the worst of it? I had a hard-on all the time I was running away. I wanted to fuck her, even though she was literally scaring me shitless and I thought she was the most disgusting thing I'd ever laid eyes on. I was fucking *desperate* for it, mate. But I was even more frightened than that.'

'I can vouch for that,' Jochen admitted. 'And I think she could have forced us if she'd wanted to, if she'd bothered chasing us. There's no way we could have outrun her. She was playing with us.'

'Not very brave of you,' grunted Hrubesch, whose earlier uncertainty seemed to have dissipated. 'You're poor specimens of Aryan manhood.'

'We never claimed to be good ones,' said Rudi. 'And quite frankly, if rubbing shoulders with a creature like that is our patriotic duty, then you can shove the fucking Third Reich up your stinking arse.'

Jochen put a hand on his friend's shoulder. 'Enough, Rudi. So how have you decided who you're going to feed to Irina to keep her sweet until we can get her back to Germany?'

'We agreed she could take whoever she likes,' said Hrubesch. 'Except for me, Berger and Karnstein, of course.'

'You sold us all to her, you arsehole?' Rudi was beside himself with fury. 'Saving your own precious skins while she…'

'For what it's worth, I believe you two are in no immediate danger. You intrigue her. She's taken a shine to you.'

'You cold fucking bastard. I should fucking end you right now.'

'Easy, Rudi,' said Jochen soothingly. 'How far to this rendezvous? And how do you know where it is?'

'I don't know the location,' Hrubesch admitted. 'Only that it's to the north and is five or six days away from here. Karnstein's taken bearings. His navigational skills are one reason he was selected for this mission. But he won't share either the rendezvous point or the contact passwords with us. It's his way of ensuring he gets there safely.'

'How noble and selfless of him,' said Jochen bitterly. 'We all die so that miserable scumbag can live. Same goes for you and Berger. Perhaps Rudi's got the right idea. Three bullets to save nearly a dozen lives.'

'Have you been listening, Hauptsturmführer? If our agreement becomes void, Irina will have us all. Believe me, this is the only way *any* of us will get home.'

'Maybe that would be for the best, Hrubesch. It would mean that *thing* won't be going to Germany. No Aryan *nosferatu* to infect the rest of the world. A dozen lives to keep millions from harm.'

Hrubesch laughed. 'Are you that brave and altruistic, Dietrich? I'd wager the death she gives would be far from quick and clean. It would be a lot worse than the death a mouse experiences when it is caught by a cat. I suspect Irina is as imaginative as she is cruel. Your choice is a simple one, Hauptsturmführer – kill us now and certainly die a terrible death, or comply with the agreement we have made and hope to live. But you had better decide quickly. Tomorrow morning we leave.'

13

Led now by Karnstein's sextant and compass rather than Hrubesch's pendulum, the dwindling column stumbled northward, constantly deviating to skirt obstructions, readjusting its course. Dressed once again as local peasant trappers, Jochen and Rudi now took up the rear, four or five metres behind the mules. They no longer cared what went on ahead of them, though they were ready to escape into the taiga if they ran into a Red Army patrol. Gunshots and screams of pain would be warning enough – though heaven knew Jochen had lately had his fill of the latter.

This was the fifth day since leaving that strange circular valley, and only five Sturmmänner remained alive. Alone in his tent, hands clapped over his ears, Jochen had heard each of the last four die – knowing what they saw, and what she was doing to them while they died, as she fed. *A praying mantis. A leech. A literal man-eater. An abomination however you looked it.* Rudi now refused to speak of her or what was happening, averting his eyes whenever she drifted into his field of vision.

And drift she did, skipping and laughing like a carefree child among the mules and the men who tended them – now including Berger, as they were a man short because Karnstein was now their guide. Sometimes she would fall in beside Jochen and talk to him.

'Your friend Rudi is a bit of a crosspatch,' she said on the morning of the first day. 'He keeps pretending I'm not there. Anyone would think I've done something to upset him.' Then she moved behind Rudi and imitated his gait, his frozen expression. After a few metres she giggled and fluttered off to mock someone else, the unwitting man who would later that night provide her entertainment. That set the pattern. She did the same three mornings running. The men noticed but could do nothing about it, caught as they were between her and whatever lethal discipline Hrubesch would mete out. No one could say they weren't warned.

Now she came skipping back to join Jochen once more. She had acquired what appeared to be a brand new white dress from somewhere, and her hair gleamed as if freshly washed, but she still stank. It was, Jochen realised, an inner corruption rather than poor hygiene – a spiritual stench, not a physical one. 'Hrubesch says we should be there by noon tomorrow,' she informed him. 'Such a shame. I've been enjoying myself. It's been a long time since I had so many playmates.'

Jochen didn't rise to her taunt. 'Why do you do behave like that? With your...' He groped for the right word. 'With your abilities you could do good, help people. Why do you kill and destroy?'

She pursed her lips. 'It's my nature,' she said. 'I was

never what you'd call a good girl. My father said I was wilful and hedonistic. Cruel, too. There was a scandal in Petersburg, so he took me to boring, boring Krasnoyarsk. He thought I might stay out of trouble there – and if not, that it was such a long way from civilisation that respectable society might not hear of it. But he soon learned the magnitude of his mistake. So there you have it, Jochen Dietrich. No sad story of corrupted maidenhood. I was already this way before I was transformed. Sammael simply gave me gifts that suited my nature. The rest is pure Irina.'

'This Sammael, you say he is present in places other than the valley – and that he can communicate with other aspects of himself across space and time. Has he told you how the war will end?'

She chuckled. 'Several different versions, actually. Apart from a few fixed and immutable points, scientific inevitabilities such as the cycles of celestial bodies and the culmination of geological or chemical processes, the future is a maze of possibilities and potential, a maze as dense and indefinable as the taiga. In human affairs, the near future is obviously easier to untangle than the longer term.'

'But if time isn't a straight line, doesn't that mean the past is also like that?'

'Sentient life is the universe's observer. As I told you, living creatures collectively give time an apparent shape, a consensus that delineates and continually informs our idea of reality. It's the only way biological life can exist within space-time, by giving it a form that contains and nurtures it. What you call the past is really the solid trail left by life as it moves through time and space. It's what you've *done*, not what you *might* do.'

'Is that what Sammael told you?'

Her smile bore more than a small trace of self-satisfaction. 'It's what I deduced from the evidence. Sammael merely confirmed it. He never lies but rarely tells the whole truth, and is a master of what you might call honest misdirection. Between you and me, I think I understand it better than he does. You may think me a monster but I'm also a scientist, and an exceptionally good one. It's all there in Einstein and Heisenberg, if you read between the lines. The observer creates her own existence simply by observing, and observation occurs through existing. Space-time is a paradox – the chicken and the egg are one and the same.'

Jochen felt a headache coming on. 'Is there one ending to the war that's more likely than any other?'

'Of course there is. But I won't spoil the surprise. Though in all fairness I should point out that it might not even happen, and if it does then it almost certainly won't be quite the way I envisage it. But does it matter? After all, one war is only a continuation of another, and they rarely unfold the same way. An anarchist's bomb in Bosnia leads to a global war, which results in humiliation and impoverishment for Germany; revolution, a dead Tsar and civil war in Russia; and the rise of Adolf Hitler, who in turn begins another overt war that ravages almost the entire world. Yet it didn't really begin with the assassination of Archduke Franz Ferdinand and it won't end with victory for one side or the other in the present phase of the endless conflict. War can be hot, war can be cold. It can be fought with bullets and bombs or business and money. It can be fought with ideas and art. If Germany loses the military struggle, it may win what follows. Whatever transpires, you will be dead and gone long before it ends.'

'Is that a threat?'

She gave him a playful nudge that turned his stomach and brought him out in gooseflesh. 'Don't be silly. I'm just saying that this is a struggle that may last, in one form or another, for another century or two, perhaps a millennium – just as its roots had their beginning long before even I was born. It isn't just about flags and nations, guns and swords, and men in uniform, you see. It is about many more things than taking sides on a battlefield and pinning silly medals on puffed-out chests. Those dramas and baubles are only tools of the men who really rule the world, although many of them don't have the faintest inkling of their power or their purpose.'

'What is their purpose?'

'Why, to control, that is all. It is the struggle for control that brings politics, economics and war into being. Evolution is not a solely biological process. But each group thinks it is striving only for its own benefit, its own survival. And that is true, but only up to a point. They do not understand how they interlock and turn together like cogs in a mechanical loom to weave the web of history – how they will determine humanity's path and create the future.'

God damn it, she sounds almost wise. For a terrible moment Jochen's revulsion was overwhelmed by the chilling absurdity of his situation. How had the social idealist and aspiring writer he had once been, living a simple but fulfilling life in an old town in Saxony, filled with dreams and ambition, metamorphosed into a jaded Waffen-SS officer who had killed his supposed comrades and was now walking and talking in broad daylight with a demonic murderess who had *eaten* his comrades, a creature any casual observer would see as nothing more than an innocent and beautiful young woman? And what was she anyway? A vampire, a cannibal, a shape-changer, a killer; all of those, without a shred of doubt. A creature made by another being that was essentially supernatural, no matter she explained its nature in quasi-scientific terms. Religion taught that the first man was transformed clay, a sculpture animated by the spark in divine breath. Irina was a further transformation, from human to monster with an infusion from Satan himself. But according to Irina, only her physical being had been affected. Her nature remained unaltered despite her biological enhancement. She possessed unnatural strength and speed, the ability to inspire both desire and dread in extremes, and that appalling power of transfiguration. But what else had been done to her?

'Are you immortal?' It was the question he almost feared to ask.

'I don't know yet. I haven't aged a day since I encountered Sammael, and I don't get sick at all. I can be injured but I heal very fast. Cuts and scratches are gone in a matter of hours. Once I fell out of a tree and broke my arm quite badly, bone sticking out and pouring with blood; but it was completely healed within a week. Didn't even need to be set or stitched. I need to eat and drink and breathe, the same as any ordinary person, though I couldn't honestly say I've tried doing without. Sometimes I think if I'm left to myself I'll probably just keep going until the sun explodes and burns the solar system to a crisp.'

'Immortality doesn't appeal to me. It would surely

become monotonous, even if everyone could have it. And if it's only for the few, the thought of outliving all my friends and loved ones, morning them through endless time...' Jochen shook his head sadly. 'I'm all for a good, long life but eternity must be very dull and lonely.'

'Variety is the spice of life, Jochen Dietrich. I like to cultivate my interests, expand my knowledge, indulge my pleasures, experiment. And I'm *very* inventive.'

She laughed delightedly, and Jochen's blood turned to ice in his veins.

That night, Rudi crawled into Jochen's tent, blanket draped around him like a cloak. 'You don't mind, do you? It's just that I don't think I can stand being alone for another night, not while I can hear – well, you know.'

'I'm glad you're here,' said Jochen. 'I feel the same way. Actually, I was about to pop over to your place.'

'Well, I was hoping your patch of ground might be a bit more comfortable than mine.' Rudi stretched out alongside Jochen and shuffled around. 'Looks like I was wrong. Oh well, I'm here now. Goodnight.' Five minutes later, he spoke again. 'I wonder which of those poor bastards she'll pick tonight?'

'Pfeiffer,' said Jochen confidently. 'She was walking behind him this morning.'

'Pfeiffer? Which one? Nose or warts?'

'Nose.'

'Bugger. This means one of us will have to look after a mule.'

'I outrank you. You know what that means.'

'Yeah,' sighed Rudi. 'It means friendship is the first

casualty of muleteering.'

'You're sounding more like your old self.'

'I suppose so. Sorry I've been keeping to myself the last few days. It's just – oh, fuck it. I don't need to spell it out. You saw what I saw, felt what I felt. Not easy to deal with. Still, at least we'll be on a plane home on the next day or so. I'd much rather face the Ivans on the Eastern Front than be here with that fucking horrible bitch.'

'No argument from me, Rudi. I expect Zhukov's lads are kicking our arses in Poland by now, but dealing with them would be a walk in the park after this. Not that I want to do any more fighting. I've had a bellyful of that – that and the Nazis.'

'Well, we are technically party members. And Waffen-SS. If we return to Germany the only way we could walk away from the Nazis is to walk toward a firing squad. If you ask me, desertion now is our only sane option.'

'We've been through this. Where could we go?'

'China,' said Rudi dreamily. 'We'd do alright there. I met some blokes who'd been there ten years or so ago, training and reorganising the Chinese military. That all went out the window when Japan invaded, of course. They were a better ally than China. Anyway, the Kuomintang and the communists are now fighting each other as well as the Japanese. I reckon the Chinese reds would just love to have a couple of highly-trained German officers as military advisors, no questions asked. Fuck, as long as they fed me and didn't make me chase vampires I'd even fight for them. At least it would be a cause we actually believe in. We might even win. Just imagine, Jochen – Chinese food all day and every day in a socialist paradise that hasn't been poisoned by a nutcase like Stalin. We could settle down, farm a bit of land and work on our writing and film-making without worrying that the Gestapo will break the bloody door down in the middle of the night. Maybe we could find a couple of nice Chinese girls. We'd be as happy as pigs in shit.'

Without warning, the night stillness was shattered by a drawn-out, high-pitched scream, followed by an agonised, wordless plea for mercy punctuated by fearful whimpers and yelps of pain, until the screaming resumed.

'That's Pfeiffer the Nose right enough,' said Rudi in a strained voice, then covered his ears with both hands and part of his blanket.

The sound of Pfeiffer's suffering continued for hours, an unrelenting cycle of crescendo and decrescendo, with subtle variations in timbre and pitch in each movement. *She's playing him like a musical instrument. Showing us what she can do.* With that thought Jochen sat up and lit a cigarette to soothe his frayed nerves. If he was going to be deprived of sleep and subjected to aural torment, he might as well have a smoke. There were only six cigarettes left in his last pack of Eckstein. He needed a fresh supply.

Guiltily, he wondered if Pfeiffer the Nose had been a smoker.

14

The river was perhaps two hundred metres wide. Fortunately, they wouldn't need to cross it, as they were already standing at Karnstein's rendezvous site, a long narrow meadow running parallel to the riverbank for around half a kilometre. Patches of charred earth and neat piles of discarded timber at one end suggested previous visitation.

'Reindeer herders,' said Irina. 'Nomads. Evenki or Ket, probably. This is pasture for their horses, grazing for their herds, though it hasn't been used for a long time. There are many such places along the river.'

'What river is this?' asked Jochen.

'The Yenisei,' she replied. 'It flows north to the Arctic Ocean. It rises in Mongolia, runs through Krasnoyarsk.'

Jochen turned to Hrubesch. 'So we could have taken a boat from Krasnoyarsk and saved ourselves a bloody long trek and a whole lot of grief?'

Hrubesch shrugged indifferently. 'We only had a rough

location and my pendulum to guide us, Hauptsturmführer. Besides, we would have been far more likely to run into Soviet forces if we'd taken the river. We couldn't afford to draw attention to our mission. Anyway, that's behind us now. Is there any point complaining about it?'

There wasn't, Jochen was forced to admit. He looked to where Karnstein was assembling the radio transmitter. It wouldn't be long now until the Abwehr man set the wheels in motion for their escape. A short distance from Karnstein, Berger was instructing the surviving Pfeiffer in the art of constructing a coffin-shaped box from prefabricated parts. That struck Jochen as an excellent idea. Perhaps one day people would be able to buy furniture that way. He imagined buying the constituent parts of a sideboard or a bed cheaply in a single flat box, ready to be collected at a shop and taken home in a car or a motorbike sidecar, where one man could put it together with nothing more than a hammer and a screwdriver. It would never catch on, though. There wasn't much glory in assembling a wardrobe.

Why had Irina agreed to allow herself to be sealed in that lead-lined box for the flight home? The lid had holes so she could breathe, but it would surely be incredibly uncomfortable. And it was unnecessary. If she restrained her – what was that word Hrubesch had used? Yes, if she bottled up her *emanations* she could pass for an ordinary young woman, at least for a time. So why did Hrubesch insist upon her entering the box, and why was Irina submitting to it?

He strolled to the riverbank and stared longingly at the water, clear in the shallows, darkening toward midstream. It had been weeks since his last bath, and he hadn't swum in several years. The nearest he'd been to total immersion in water had been that unbelievable downpour back on the trail, when his clothing and every centimetre of his body had been drenched. But rain wasn't the same as either a swim in cold water or a good long soak in a hot tub. In any case, rain just wasn't the same anymore. Nowadays it always felt dirty with smoke and ashes from blasted and burning cities, particles from shredded and roasted corpses carried into the upper atmosphere on pressures waves and convection, only to absorb water vapour and fall again as greasy, wet droplets. If the Yenisei started in Mongolia, would that mean its water was cleaner than that which fell from the sky? Perhaps it was fed by tributaries that began in the Altai mountain range or the Himalayas, ancient water from glaciers and old, old snow. Rudi would know, with his love of physical geography. But Rudi was busy with the mules and the river was *there*.

In a kind of trance, Jochen sat and took off his battered workman's boots with their worn heels and thinning soles, then stood and removed first his jacket, then his shirt and trousers, leaving only his stained and threadbare cotton drawers. He looked sadly down at his torso. *My ribs and collarbone never used to stick out like that, and I'm sure I had the beginnings of a beer belly. Where did I go?* He took a deep breath and walked into the water, wading until the river came up to his chest. He stopped there for a few seconds, panting and shivering, then took one deep breath and went on until the Yenisei covered him completely.

Something brushed against him, turned and nuzzled cautiously at his arm. Jochen opened his eyes to see a big fish disappearing into the murk. A sturgeon. There were other, smaller fish – he recognised perch and dace – pieces of driftwood that might have travelled all the way from Mongolia, a sodden page from a newspaper with washed-out Cyrillic script. He glimpsed one word before the sheet was borne out of sight by the current: Сталин. Stalin's name, voyaging inexorably toward the polar ice, to the region so sacred to all those deranged Nazi ideas about the origins of the Aryan race. It felt like an omen. All the world's seas, rivers, lakes and streams were connected in one way or another – clouds, rain and snow, too. It was like that maze of time and possibility Irina had spoken of, a vast and intricate web of decisions and processes. Now, Jochen saw Stalin's fire converging on Aryan ice, the primal conflict of Hanns Hörbiger's *Welteislehre* theory that so many Germans now believed in, an idea that was self-evidently preposterous. A perfect delusion for a people in the grip of an insane vanity.

The Third Reich would crumble to nothing, crushed between the British and Americans to the west, the Soviet Union to the east. Germany would burn and its people would suffer as they had caused others to suffer. That defeat had begun the moment Adolf Hitler had been appointed chancellor. He and his cronies had turned Germany into a rabid dog, snarling and snapping at its neighbours, biting and bullying and worrying at the whole world, spreading its murderous disease across the globe. It was only right that it should be put down. But, for ordinary, decent Germans, those who hated the Nazi regime but were too weak, powerless and fearful to act, the cure would be as bad as the sickness. In his mind's eye, Jochen saw Berlin burning, Soviet tanks crawling like angry cockroaches among the rubble, the Ivans swarming through its shattered streets like soldier ants, destroying everything, killing everyone in their path.

His Leipzig had already gone, bombed and all but destroyed by the Allies the previous December. Yet it had been disappearing slowly before that, the large Jewish population evicted, forced out, then deported to the camps at Auschwitz, Buchenwald and Theresienstadt. In ten years, eleven thousand Jews had become zero. On his last visit, for his mother's funeral a couple of months before the firestorm, the city's character had changed completely, its synagogues and many of its shops and factories torched and gutted. Jochen's kindly Jewish neighbours and childhood friends vanished forever. His father, the god-fearing Lutheran minister, had gloated over the Jews' departure, ranting from the pulpit with his moustache newly sculpted in imitation of his earthly Saviour, somehow contriving to blame the Jews for his wife's death from a stroke. Jochen had not been back or made contact since, fervently but guiltily hoping his hypocrite father had died in the bombing. There was nothing left for him in the blackened ruins of Leipzig. He could never go home.

Jochen closed his eyes, opened his mouth, spread his arms and let the cold current carry him into the deep, into the dark.

'You fucking idiot,' Rudi raged. 'What were you thinking? If it hadn't been for *her* you'd be fuck knows where up the river by now and probably fucking *dead*.'

Jochen blinked water from his eyes. 'I just went for a swim,' he protested. 'Wanted to clean up a bit. Must have got out of my depth.'

'Bollocks. You can swim like a fucking fish. What happened out there?'

'Nothing, honestly. I think I might have fallen asleep. Just nodded off.'

'Fallen asleep? Arseholes. That water's like fucking ice. Nobody could just *nod off* in that.'

Jochen frowned. 'I must have done, but I can't really remember. How did I get out?'

'That bitch spotted you heading downstream, jumped in and hauled your stupid arse out.' Rudi jerked a thumb over his shoulder to where Irina, stark naked but seemingly oblivious of the fact, had hung her dress to dry over a bush lush with red, translucent berries and was dancing around it, singing in a sweet, clear voice that set Jochen's teeth on edge. 'She's been singing that bloody "clinker" song since she pulled you out of the water,' Rudi grumbled. 'It's really getting on my tits.'

'Have I been unconscious that long?'

'No, only a couple of minutes, but with that racket it seems much longer. You know, this must be the first time in human history that an attractive young woman has danced in the altogether slap bang in the middle of a bunch of hairy-arsed soldiers and none of them have so much as had a sly peek. Not even me.'

'If you didn't look, how did you know?'

'Ah, you've got me there. A conditioned reflex, I suppose – like Pavlov's dog, only with women undressing instead of a bell ringing. But you can take it from me that no one else has had an eyeful. They're all shitting themselves in case she works up an appetite with all that prancing around.'

'You don't seem too worried.'

'There's a bullet in my Luger if she comes anywhere near me.'

'I don't think that would stop Irina.'

'I never said the bullet was for her, mate.'

Jochen had no rejoinder for that. After all, hadn't he been thinking along the same lines during the past few days? He rose and walked to where he'd left his clothes, and began to dress. As he was buttoning his shirt, Irina appeared, still naked. Out of habit, Jochen averted his eyes, though evidently she didn't give a damn about modesty – or maybe she simply knew that nobody would dare look, and certainly not more than once.

'You saved me,' he said. 'I should thank you.' It was a formal expression of a gratitude he didn't really feel.

'I was ready,' she said. 'As soon as I saw you by the river I knew you would do that. Your life weighs heavily upon you, Jochen Dietrich. You crave sleep.'

'Then why didn't you let me drown?'

She sighed. 'Because this isn't where you end. Do you know why I hate the Bolsheviks so much? Not because they killed the Romanovs. I couldn't care less about that. No, it is because they think strength is beauty and history is worthless; because all they care about is production and its glorification. For them the natural world is merely a source of food and raw materials, a thing to be worked. Art has no purpose other than to inspire more work. And they do not understand that when the proletariat becomes its own tyrant, the workers will turn on one another, and on themselves. The Bolsheviks are ignorant peasants who are convinced their narrowness of vision and uneducated dourness are true images of the world. They are so chained to their hammers and sickles that they have forgotten how to put them down and *live*. I know what I am, Jochen – a monster in your eyes and my own. I have always been one, from the instant of my conception. But sometimes I dance and sing and lose myself among the lovely trees. Even though they shun me, I marvel from afar at the flight of birds and the grace of tigers and deer, wolves and horses, the tenderness of all beasts toward their young. I do these things to forget what I am, just for a few wonderful moments. The Bolsheviks never forget what they are. They never put down their tools, not even when they go to sleep at night. And their tools are no longer shovels and ploughs but human beings.'

'The Nazis are as bad. Worse.'

'Yes, I know. My conversations with Hrubesch have taught me that much. Hrubesch and the others – they are worse than the Bolsheviks. People who have industrialised murder, who revel in torture and butchery and believe it is for the greater good. Men who believe their own base urges to be the yardstick of morality, and whose laws benefit only themselves. Liars and masters of self-deception. Monsters who think they are righteous men, destiny's chosen, the self-elected, blood-drenched saints of the Third Reich.'

'Then why on earth did you agree to go with them to Germany?'

'Because Sammael told me that is where I shall die at last, surrounded by the evil they have created, an evil I could never hope to match even in my most ferocious and bloody dreams.' She smiled sadly. 'Until then I cannot do otherwise than act in accordance with my nature. I must, if I am to play my part in shaping what is to unfold many years from now.'

Jochen stared at her, feeling pity in spite of his revulsion, in spite of all the dreadful things she had done. She was the epitome of paradox: beautiful yet corrupt; vicious but understanding; both brutal and sensitive. And she was indeed wise, fully cognisant of what she was, hating the horrors she inflicted and at the same time revelling in them. A tragic, damaged creature who didn't care whether or not she deserved to live, but who was content in the foreknowledge of her death. His heart, unbelievably, went out to her.

Unexpectedly, she reached up and tenderly stroked his cheek. 'There. That is what I see in you, Jochen Dietrich. A man who looks beyond surfaces, who wants to know the heart of things, who can feel as others feel. You are not like the men who surround you, and though you believe yourself a socialist, neither you are like the Bolsheviks. That is why I shall never harm you. Nor will I harm Rudi Brandt, because he is your friend. And I suppose he is rather entertaining.' She frowned and took her hand away. 'True purity must always be flawed. Sammael is twinned with Atem, his polar opposite; but in essence they are a unity and we ourselves determine which aspect manifests in our presence. They are two fruits of the same tree: one bitter, the other sweet. Yet they reflect the essence of humanity. There is a spark of Sammael in Atem and a spark of Atem in Sammael. In the same way, there is a hint of darkness deep inside you, just as there is a tiny flicker of light within me. Opposites attract but like calls to like. The eternal paradox of the human heart, that volatile and dangerous organ, so vital yet so deadly. I have never known whether to despise its poison or yearn for it, so of course I do neither and both — another paradox. "Sorrow is knowledge: they who know the most must mourn the deepest o'er the fatal truth, the Tree of Knowledge is not that of Life." I value knowledge above all else. If I cannot know one thing, then I shall know another.'

'You don't have to die,' he said, not understanding what she was trying to say but uncomfortable with the direction it seemed to be taking. 'You could go back into the taiga. Surely you can find another way to live? Hunt animals instead of men, eat fruit and vegetables like a normal person.'

'By choice I have not eaten any meat but man since I was altered. The beasts in the fields and forest should exist in peace, without fear of anything but what nature brings. Roots and berries, nuts and leaves do not nourish me. Besides, I must go to Germany. That is why I shall submit to their little box tonight, the box they want me to enter because they cannot bear my presence and foolishly think a thin sheet of lead will make it easier to endure. Not because I endorse the Nazi cause or agree with their infantile notions of racial purity. Nor because I hate the Bolsheviks. Nor even because if all men and women were like me, there would be no one left to write the poems. No, I go for one reason only. My death will come about when I deliver a message to those who need to hear it.'

'What will that message be?'

'A warning to the future. That I exist. That creatures like me *can* exist.'

She stepped backward into the shadow of a tree and vanished, reappearing almost instantaneously by the berry-laden bush on which her dress was drying, singing that maddening song again. It was only then that he realised the itching and buzzing inside his skull had stopped – and that for one brief moment the noxious stench that perpetually enveloped Irina had been replaced by the sweet scent of cinnamon.

15

At almost exactly three o'clock the next morning they watched the plane circle, visible only as a silhouette against the stars, then begin its descent as soon as Karnstein lit the makeshift landing lights. Irina was in her lead-lined box, loudly humming that annoying song, with Hrubesch and Berger standing stiffly at either end like a guard of honour. The Sturmmänner were doing as instructed, throwing the remaining firearms and ammunition into the Yenisei and making a pile of their tents, rucksacks and bags. Unnecessary weight, Hrubesch said, was dangerous weight. All they would be taking were the clothes they wore.

'I don't like this,' said Rudi. 'If the Ivans turn up now we'll be caught with our trousers down and our arses hanging out. They should have let the men hold on to their MP 40s until the bloody plane landed.'

'Too late now,' said Jochen. 'You should stop worrying. We'll be in the air in ten minutes. What with stops for rest and refuelling, I reckon this time tomorrow

I'll be persuading the pilot to drop us off somewhere near Stockholm.'

'Good luck with that.'

'I'm sure my little metal friend Herr Luger will be most persuasive.'

'You kept yours? You sly bastard.'

'And you didn't?'

Rudi grinned and patted his jacket pocket. 'What do you think?'

'I knew I could rely on you for an elastic interpretation of orders. Two will be better than one. Karnstein's bound to have something up his sleeve, and his Ivan mates are sure to have guns.'

The aircraft made a bumpy but safe landing. When the hatch opened, Karnstein hurried over and spoke to the pilot, then waved to Hrubesch, who ordered the remaining four Sturmmänner to carry the box over to the plane.

'Karnstein still has his MP 40,' said Jochen. 'That's not good. Let's hope he ditches it before we board.'

Rudi tugged urgently at his sleeve. 'Jochen, that fucking plane's a Yakoviev Yak-6. It won't take all of us.'

'What? But it looks big enough.'

'The cockpit holds a pilot and co-pilot. They're already aboard, right? Other than that there are four seats behind the cockpit and a bit of space for cargo. The Yak-6 can only take up to five hundred kilos weight in passengers or cargo.'

'How the hell do you know that?'

'I like planes. And I pay attention in briefings, unlike some people I could mention. The point is, there are ten of us, plus Irina in that heavy box, which must weigh nearly as much as two men, more with her in it. Do the sums,

Jochen. Hrubesch, Berger and Karnstein – and the box? About five hundred kilos altogether I'd say, give or take. Those fuckers are going to leave the rest of us behind.'

By now, the box was safely stowed in the plane and Hrubesch and Berger were climbing aboard. Jochen drew his Luger and started toward the plane, Rudi hard at his heels. They came to an abrupt halt when Karnstein turned and aimed his MP 40 at them.

'You two, stay where you are. You Sturmmänner by the plane, get your arses over here. And be quick about it.'

'You bastard motherfucking arsehole, Karnstein,' Rudi hissed. 'I hope she eats you alive and shits you out somewhere over Finland.'

'Nothing personal, Brandt,' Karnstein's eyes told a different story. His shoulders twitched, as much of a shrug as he could be bothered to muster. 'Orders are orders. Mine are to leave no personnel behind to be interrogated. Somehow I don't think the Reich can trust any of you to take your cyanide pills like proper SS men.'

With that, he turned to the four Sturmmänner and fired around half the bullets from the MP 40s magazine into them, the noise barely audible above the sound of the aircraft engines. The men jerked backward and cried out as they fell, but only the Pfeiffer the Wart was still alive when he hit the ground. Karnstein finished him off with the remaining bullets, slotting home a replacement magazine before the shocked Jochen and Rudi had a chance to move a muscle. Then he pointed the submachine gun at them, only to lower it slightly when Rudi began to laugh. 'What's so damned funny?'

Rudi merely waved a hand and kept on laughing. A

mirthless smile crept across Jochen's face. 'You wouldn't understand, Karnstein, but we're sort of back where we started, only the jackboot's on the other foot. Let's just say it's good to know that the universe has a sense of humour.'

Karnstein muttered something and raised the MP 40 again. Rudi continued to laugh. Jochen looked Karnstein in the eye. *Go on then. Do it. Get it over with.*

But only a single shot came. Jochen flinched, surprised that he felt no pain, and slightly irritated that Rudi was apparently unharmed and still cackling uncontrollably. Then he saw that most of Karnstein's forehead was now a shapeless hole, his lower face a mask of blood, bone fragments and puréed brain tissue.

The Abwehr man's eyes rolled wildly and his reddened lips moved soundlessly. The MP 40 fell to the ground released by fingers that now had no brain to control them. Karnstein managed to take one step forward before his legs buckled and he collapsed like a broken marionette, blood quickly pooling around his ruined head. Jochen looked up to see Berger leaning out of the plane's hatch, Hrubesch's Walther in his hand.

Berger nodded once and disappeared from view. The hatch closed and the aircraft began its take-off. Jochen was tempted to put a bullet or two its way, but decided against it. One of the passengers had her own mission to complete, and he wouldn't stand in her way.

'Well, so much for Sweden,' said Rudi, his laughter banished. 'What the fuck just happened?'

'Berger just saved our lives, Rudi.'

'That's bloody decent of him,' said Rudi disgustedly. 'He lets that arsehole Karnstein kill the other blokes, then tops Karnstein to save us? Where's the logic in that? Maybe him and Hrubesch never intended to take any of us back with them. But in that case, why not kill us?'

'It was a compromise. He had to obey orders but he's afraid of Irina. I think she worked out what they were up to and told him not to harm us, or else they'd get more than just a bumpy ride home.'

'Well, I'll be buggered. The mad cannibal makes one treacherous bastard save us from another treacherous bastard. Just when I was thinking my life couldn't possibly get any weirder. Got a cigarette?'

Jochen took the remaining cigarettes from the pack and tossed the empty carton away.

'Shit,' said Rudi as they lit up. 'Are these the last two?'

'We should be okay for a while. Most of the others smoked so I'm sure there will be a pack or two in that pile of bags over there. I'm going to smoke Karnstein's first. I might even blow a smoke-ring or two into what's left of his face.'

'You spiteful sod. Can I piss on him first?'

'You can do whatever you want, Rudi. I really don't care anymore. Dignity and decency are things of the past. What the war hasn't taken from us, this mission has. We've been stripped of everything that makes us human. Irina was right – she's a monster but the Third Reich is worse. And we're part of it, no matter how much we hate it. What we did at Babi Yar means nothing because after that we should have done more to stop the madness. The Reich is a darkness deeper than any night the world has ever known, and it's getting darker by the day. Do we deserve to stand in the light? Have we earned that right?'

Rudi stared at his friend's anguished face. He'd never seen Jochen so miserable, so tormented. 'We're just two blokes who wanted to do the right thing and stay alive at the same time,' he said quietly. 'We saved some Jews and we've tried not to kill or hurt anyone else. We did some good and we haven't done anything really bad. We're not saints, Jochen, and we're not avenging angels; but we're definitely not devils. It's true that we've made a couple of piss-poor decisions – like joining the fucking SS and the damned Nazis in the first place – but in our own way we've made an effort not to compound those mistakes. I know that when history judges us there will be no one to speak for us. We'll only ever be thought of as two more SS thugs out of thousands, and the world will assume we'll be shuffling off to eternal damnation with the rest. But we know that isn't what we are, so we shouldn't feel guilty for what other people have done or for what we couldn't do. If our best wasn't good enough, that wasn't our fault. We just found ourselves in a very bad place at the worst possible time.'

'But we've lost everything, Rudi. Even our future. I feel as though I'm in a long tunnel and I can't see a light at the end.'

'Actually, there is a bright side. We have the mules, a couple of guns, a few knives, tents and blankets, and what's left of the rations. And we have a hammer, a saw, a screwdriver and a bag of nails and screws left over from putting that box together. I mean, look at all these trees. We could build a boat.'

'A boat? Are you serious?'

'Alright then, a raft. Oars or paddles, too. A bit of a

shelter to keep the rain off. We could row it south toward Krasnoyarsk, pick up the horses and get our arses out of this fucking war. It's got to be easier than walking. Or if you like we could stay here, build a cabin and live off the land, breed mules. On second thoughts, maybe not that. You'd need to be either completely bloody mad or totally sick of life to live in this bastard place. Besides, I wouldn't trust Irina to keep her hands off us for too long. She'd have you for breakfast, mate. And I mean that literally. God only knows what she'd do to a good-looking boy like me. Mind you, I might be a bit of a disappointment, what with all the chafing.'

'She won't be coming back to Siberia,' said Jochen. 'You can trust me on that. It's strange but I wish I'd had a chance to say goodbye, but I didn't see her after she pulled me out of the river.'

'Say goodbye? Jochen, she's a fucking murderer, a cannibal. Worse that that, she's the closest thing to a demon we're ever likely to meet.' Rudi paused, eyes round with horror. 'Shit, don't tell me you…?'

'No, nothing like that, you idiot. Believe it or not, I feel sorry for her. Don't ask me why. I couldn't explain it in a month of Sundays.'

'Even so, in a couple of days she'll be in Germany. I dread to think what she'll do there. Mengele and the other bloke will have no idea what they're dealing with. And as for those poor sods in whichever camp they'll give her to play with… ' Rudi shook his head dolefully.

'It could be a lot worse. Irina thinks she'll die there. Besides, Hrubesch and Berger have made a big mistake. They were too fixated on the prize in front of them, so intent on taking Irina that they completely ignored or forgot about Sammael, whoever or whatever that might be. Or maybe they simply didn't believe what Irina told them.'

'I'm not sure I did,' Rudi frowned. 'It sounded like madness to me.'

'She never lied to us, Rudi. Not once. Why believe everything else but not that?'

'Because it's crazy?'

'No crazier than believing in a shape-changing, superhuman, immortal cannibal who can travel by going into one shadow and emerging from another a mile away.'

'When you put it that way...' Rudi shrugged, then frowned. 'So you're saying they took the creation but left the creator behind.'

'Exactly. Which is one very good reason to get as far away from this place as we can.' Jochen shook himself. 'In any case, whatever Sammael might be, I don't fancy staying here anyway. It'll be a while yet before any game animals return, and I am not eating our mules, not after the service they've given us. And you can't breed them anyway.'

'Why not?'

'Well, in the first place, mules are usually infertile. And secondly, ours are all female. Though I suppose you could do the honours if you think it's worth a try.'

Rudi pensively stroked his chin. 'Ah. That complicates matters slightly. And although I have grown rather fond of the beasts over the past weeks, there are limits to even my sense of duty. In which case I'd better just turn them loose.'

'Anyway, mules or no mules, I really do not want to be living in a log cabin during a Siberian winter. I want a place with fewer bloody trees, somewhere we're not likely to be arrested and shot. Somewhere warmer, with decent washing facilities and good food and beer.'

'Well, that's settled then,' said Rudi cheerfully as he made a bee-line for the dead men's baggage. 'China, here we come.'

Jochen smiled as he watched his friend gleefully ransack the heap of backpacks and bags. Rudi was surely the most optimistic misery guts the human species had ever produced. However much Rudi bitched and complained it was only because he firmly believed that things could and should be better than they were, and knew without a shadow of doubt that they would be better once all the idiots, incompetents and arseholes were removed from the equation. It was hard to argue with that assessment. Maybe it was time Jochen took a leaf out of Rudi's book.

He looked up at the sky. To the east, the stars were dimming and a faintly glowing arch softened the near-black horizon, though it was more than an hour until the sun was due to come up. The zodiacal light, the sun's rays reflected and scattered by a vast, elliptical cloud of interplanetary dust; the phenomenon people called a false dawn. Perhaps that's exactly what it was – an ersatz sunrise fitting for a world that had become the playground of lies and delusion. But still, it was light, and proof enough that somewhere there was more.

Author's Note

A Deeper Darkness is a prequel to both 'The Beautiful Beast' (in *A Yellow Room*) and *The Gorgon's Daughters*, but has connections with all the books in the *Havensea/Wonderland Investigations* sequence and associated stories.

While this is a work of fiction, it does have some roots in historical fact. The ethnic Germans or 'Swabians' who fled the Balkans in the early 1940s did indeed report blood-drinking and bestially aggressive behaviour in various individuals, explicitly described as vampires, among the Yugoslav partisans, as described in the story (see Eric Kurlander, *Hitler's Monsters: a Supernatural History of the Third Reich*, 2017). Refusal by members of the SS to carry out executions could be punished by imprisonment. Given the nature of the SS it is not surprising that refusal was rare and, if it did happen, usually associated with what we would now call Post-traumatic Stress Disorder arising from previous participation in executions rather than upfront conscientious objection (see Daniel Goldhagen, 'The "cowardly" executioner: On disobedience in the SS', *Patterns of Prejudice* 19:2, 1985). VIEM, the USSR's All Union Institute of Experimental Medicine, really existed and was involved in some very weird research (see Andrei Znamenski, *Red Shambhala: Magic, Prophecy, and Geopolitics in the Heart of Asia*, 2011).

Most historians agree that there is no evidence for the existence of the Vril Society, which was first mentioned in *Le Matin des magiciens* by Louis Pauwels and Jacques Bergier, a highly speculative exploration of pseudoscience and occultism published in 1960. However, a group that possibly called itself Wahrheitsgesellschaft was concerned with investigating Vril, according to a 1947 article by the German rocket engineer Willy Ley ('Pseudoscience in Naziland' in *Astounding Science Fiction*); and in 1930 a short book titled *Vril. Die Kosmische Urkraft* by 'Johannes Täufer' appeared, its pseudonymous author claiming to be a member of a secret group called Reichsarbeitsgemeinschaft. Whether either of these was the model for the Vril Society claimed by Pauwels and Bergier is debatable, but they at least demonstrate that obscure or secretive groups were (or were believed to be) actively studying Vril in the Nazi era. On the other hand, absence of evidence is not evidence of absence. Pauwels and Bergier (who played fast and loose with facts) claimed the Vril Society was a secretive inner circle of the very real and documented (not to mention highly influential) Thule Society. Anyway, what's the point of a secret society everybody knows about?

All characters with speaking parts or mentioned as their off-stage friends or relatives are fictitious. All other people mentioned in the story are real historical figures, except Hans Vögel (who appears in name only in my novel *The Gorgon's Daughters* and has no relation to the real-life German politician or the scientist of the same name); the stage magician the Amazing Rotwang, named after the sinister inventor in Fritz Lang's 1927 film *Metropolis* (and its literary source, Thea von Harbou's 1925 novel of the same name); while Josef Mengele's fictitious collaborator Sieben Pretorius is a version of the scientist Septimus Pretorius in James Whale's 1935 film *The Bride of Frankenstein* (the dialogue on page 116 includes a line lifted from the film).

Der Giftpilz (The Poisonous Mushroom or *The Toadstool)* is a 1938 children's book by Julius Streicher with illustrations by Philipp Rupprecht. It portrays Jews as child-molesters and brutal employers, propagates the Blood Libel, and includes fake quotes from the Talmud. Bearing in mind that this toxic brew was aimed at kids, anti-Semitism doesn't get much worse. The 1940 film *Jud Süß* (*Süss the Jew*) runs it pretty close, though. Approved by Goebbels, it was based in part on a novel by the Jewish author Lion Feuchtwanger, about Joseph Süß Oppenheimer (financial advisor to Duke Karl Alexander of Württemberg in the early 1700s), which was originally a study of both human weakness and anti-Semitism. *Der Große Liebe* (*The Great Love*, 1942) is another propaganda film, in which love conquers all and so do the Nazis.

On page 32, *Lasciate ogne speranza, voi ch'intrate* is the famous 'Abandon all hope, you who enter here' inscribed over the gates of hell in Dante's *Inferno*; and *Arbeit macht frei* is the infamous slogan 'Work makes you free' seen on the gates of Auschwitz, Dachau, Sachsenhausen and other Nazi concentration camps.

The lines quoted by Irina on page 110 are from Revelation 8:10-11; those on page 113 are from *The Flower That Smiles Today* by Percy Bysshe Shelley (*Posthumous Poems*, 1824); and those on page 139 are from Byron's *Manfred, a dramatic poem* (1817).

The 'clinker' song mentioned on page 135 is the well-known Russian piece 'Kalinka', composed by Ivan Larionov in 1860. Калинка/*kalinka* is an affectionate form of калина/*kalina*, the Russian name for *Viburnum opulus*, better known as the guelder rose, which is the bush on which Irina dries her dress. Its attractive translucent red fruits – berries are associated with eroticism in Russian tradition – are edible in small amounts but mildly toxic and can cause vomiting and diarrhoea.

Although all but one of the characters in *A Deeper Darkness* is German, all dialogue is given 'in translation', as it were, as Standard or colloquial English. However, I have used the German names for certain foods, commercially-produced items, weapons, military ranks, and a few other things. A glossary is provided below.

Finally, you may question the wisdom of portraying SS officers, generally regarded as the epitome of human evil, as sympathetic characters. My reasons are in the story.

Alby Stone
Walworth, London
December 2018

Glossary

Abwehr: Nazi military intelligence.

Ahnenerbe: Nominally a branch of the SS, the Ahnenerbe combined science with mysticism to both explore and justify Nazi racial theory. It conducted several known scientific and archaeological expeditions abroad before the outbreak of war in 1939, which forced the cancellation of several others.

Bratapfel: Baked apple.

Erbswurst: A sausage-shaped roll of dehydrated pea soup in tablet form, issued to German troops as iron rations from the 1870 Franco-Prussian war onward.

Flak: A German anti-aircraft gun. The name has become synonymous with the airbursts of anti-aircraft shells.

Fliegenpilz: The fly agaric mushroom.

Franzbrötchen: Cinnamon pastry, fillings vary.

Gestapo: An abbreviation of 'Geheime Staatspolizei' (Secret State Police), the secret police of Nazi Germany and occupied Europe

Hauptsturmführer: The Waffen-SS rank equivalent to a captain.

Horst Wessel Lied: A song commemorating Nazi 'martyr' Horst Wessel, a leader of the Nazi paramilitary Sturmabteilung in Berlin who was murdered by communists in 1930.

Korn: A traditional German distilled liquor.

Krampus: A demonic, goat-like companion of St Nicholas in Bavaria, Austria and neighbouring countries, who punishes misbehaving children in the Christmas season.

The stick to Santa's festive carrot.

Milbenkäse: 'Mite cheese', so called because it is ripened by the digestive juices of cheese mites, *Tyrophagus casei*.

MP 40: The submachine gun popularly but erroneously known as the Schmeisser, manufactured by the Erfurter Maschinenfabrik company.

Nollendorfplatz: A gay district of Berlin in the 1920s and early 1930s.

Oberleutnant: The rank of senior lieutenant in the Wehrmacht.

Obersturmführer: The Waffen-SS rank equivalent to Oberleutnant.

Panzer: A tank.

Pfifferling: The chanterelle mushroom.

Raumkraft: 'Spatial energy', a hypothetical force which the Austrian inventor Karl Schappeller claimed could be used to power machines.

Reichsarbeitsgemeinschaft: The 'Empire Association', a minor esoteric group in Weimar-era Germany, thought by some to be another name for the probably non-existent Vril Society.

Schneckennudeln: Spiral cinnamon rolls.

Schollen-roman: 'Novel of the soil', a popular literary genre based on nationalistic ideas from the late 1800s, promoting racialist and rural values, and a romantic and mystical union of German blood with German soil.

Schutzstaffel: The SS as a corporate entity.

Sicherheitsdienst: The intelligence arm of the SS and the Nazi party, the Sicherheitsdienst des Reichsführers-SS.

Skat: A card game popular in parts of Germany.

Sturmmann (plural **Sturmmänner**): The Waffen-SS rank

equivalent to a private.

Ursprungzellen: Literally 'origin cells'. An imaginary early discovery of stem cells. Here it refers to both embryonic stem cells and adult progenitor cells. The real Mengele did not discover these.

Volksursprüngegesellschaft: The 'Folk Origins Society'. To the best of my knowledge this has no existence outside these pages.

Wahrheitsgesellschaft: The 'Society for Truth', the original name of the Vril Society, according to Nazi rocket scientist Willy Ley.

Wandervogel: One of several German youth movements similar to the Scouts, suppressed by the Nazis in 1933.

Wehrmacht: The regular army of Nazi Germany.

Weihnachtsmann: Father Christmas.

Welteislehre: The 'World Ice theory' proposed by Austrian engineer Hanns Hörbiger (following a visionary experience in 1894) with German amateur astronomer Philipp Fauth. Hörbiger and Fauth thought the solar system had been created when a dead star saturated with water crashed into a much larger active star. The resulting explosion threw the water into space, where it froze into vast blocks of ice to form other solar systems and the Milky Way. Hörbiger sneered at Einstein and relativity, belittled calculations that proved him wrong, claimed that photographs of the Milky Way showing billions of stars had been faked, treated critics of his ideas as personal enemies, and didn't think much of Newton. Reputedly, Hitler and Himmler were big fans.

About the Author

Alby Stone was born and grew up in Southend-on-Sea in Essex, but he has lived and worked in London for many years. He is the author of several works of non-fiction, and various novels and short stories.

For news, views and free-to-read short fiction allegedly by Alby Stone and other writers, visit:

http://www.vaingloriouslunacy.com

More fiction by Alby Stone

The Forgotten Stars
Secret Songs
The Hand of Fire
(The *Havensea* trilogy)

The Sorrows of Angels
The Shadow Woman
Disappearer
Intruder
The Gorgon's Daughters
(The *Wonderland Investigations* series)

A Yellow Room
Third Sight
(Prequels to the *Havensea* and *Wonderland Investigations* series)

Cherry Blood
Dummy
A Single Drop of Night
The Girl in the Tie-Dye Dress
Fox
Woodwise
The Canaanite
House of Dust
Nocturne
The Midnight Lamp
The Lantern men

Sparks and Ashes: Short Fiction
Possibly Dangerous: Short Fiction

Available from
The Clerkenwell Writers Asylum

The Clerkenwell Writers Asylum First Short Story Collection

The Clerkenwell Writers Asylum Second Short Story Collection

Morbid and Disgusting Tales: More Short Stories from the Clerkenwell Writers Asylum

For short stories, articles and further information, visit:

https://clerkenwellwritersasylum.wordpress.com

Printed in Great Britain
by Amazon